PENGUIN BOOKS

Rumpole and the Primrose Path

Sir John Mortimer is a playwright, novelist and former practising barrister. His novels include the Leslie Titmuss trilogy, about the rise of an ambitious Tory MP: *Paradise Postponed, Titmuss Regained* and *The Sound of Trumpets*, as well as various Rumpole titles, most recently *Rumpole Rests His Case* and *Rumpole and the Primrose Path*. He has also written three volumes of autobiography, including *The Summer of a Dormouse*, which was published to great critical acclaim and became a bestseller in 2000. All these books are available in Penguin.

Sir John lives in what was once his father's house in the Chilterns. He received a knighthood for his services to the arts in the 1998 Queen's birthday honours list.

John Mortimer

Rumpole and the Primrose Path

PENGUIN BOOKS

PENGUIN BOOKS

Published by the Penguin Group
Penguin Books Ltd, 80 Strand, London WC2R 0RL, England
Penguin Putnam Inc., 375 Hudson Street, New York, New York 10014, USA
Penguin Books Australia Ltd, 250 Camberwell Road,
Camberwell, Victoria 3124, Australia
Penguin Books Canada Ltd, 10 Alcorn Avenue, Toronto, Ontario, Canada M4V 3B2
Penguin Books India (P) Ltd, 11 Community Centre,
Panchsheel Park, New Delhi – 110 017, India
Penguin Books (NZ) Ltd, Cnr Rosedale and Airborne Roads,
Albany, Auckland, New Zealand
Penguin Books (South Africa) (Pty) Ltd, 24 Sturdee Avenue,
Rosebank 2196, South Africa

Penguin Books Ltd, Registered Offices: 80 Strand, London WC2R 0RL, England

www.penguin.com

First published by Viking 2002
Published in Penguin Books 2003
1

Set in Monotype Plantin
Printed in England by Clays Ltd, St Ives plc

For Kathy Lette

'Do not, as some ungracious pastors do,
Show me the steep and thorny way to heaven,
Whiles, like a puff'd and reckless libertine,
Himself the primrose path of dalliance treads'

Shakespeare, *Hamlet*,
Act I, Scene 3

'I had thought to have let in
some of all professions that go the primrose
way to the everlasting bonfire.'

Shakespeare, *Macbeth*,
Act 2, Scene 3

Contents

Rumpole and the
Primrose Path

The regular meeting of the barristers who inhabit my old Chambers in Equity Court took place, one afternoon, in an atmosphere of particular solemnity. Among those present was a character entirely new to them, a certain Luci Gribble, whom our leader, in a momentary ambition to reach the status of an 'entrepreneur', had taken on as Director of Marketing and Administration.

Mizz Liz Probert, observing the scene, later described Luci (why she had taken to this preposterous spelling of the name of Wordsworth's great love was clear to nobody) as in her thirties, with a 'short bob', referring to hair which was not necessarily as blonde as it seemed, a thin nose, slightly hooded eyes and a determined chin. She wore a black trouser suit and bracelets clinked at her wrists. The meeting was apparently interrupted from time to time, as she gave swift instructions to the mobile phone she kept in her jacket pocket. She also wore high-heeled black boots which Liz Probert priced at not far short of three hundred pounds.

'I'm vitally concerned with the profile of Equity Court.' Luci had a slight northern accent and a way, Liz noticed, of raising her voice at the end of her sentence, so every statement sounded like a question. 'I take it that it's in the parameters of my job description to include the field of public relations and the all-important question of the company's – that is to say' (here Liz swears that Luci corrected herself reluctantly) 'the *Chambers'* image. Correct, Chair?'

This was an undoubted question, but it seemed to be addressed to an article of furniture, one of that old dining-room set, now much mended and occasionally wobbly, which had been bequeathed to Equity Court in the will of C. H. Wystan, my wife Hilda's father and once Head of our Chambers. However, Soapy Sam Ballard, as our present Head and so chairman of the meeting, appeared to follow the new arrival's drift.

'Of course that's your job, Luci.' Soapy Sam was on Christian-name terms with the woman who called him Chair. 'To improve our image. That's why we hired you. After all, we don't want to be described as a group of old fuddy-duddies, do we?' Chair, who might be thought by some to fit the description perfectly, smiled round at the meeting.

'It's not so much the fuddy-duddy label that concerns me at the moment, although I shall be including that in a future presentation. It's the heartless thing that worries me.'

'Heartless?' Ballard was puzzled.

'The public image of barristers,' Luci told the meeting, 'equals money-grabbing fat cats, insincere defenders of clients who are obviously guilty, chauvinists and outdated wig-wearing shysters.'

'Did you say "shysters"?' Claude Erskine-Brown, usually mild mannered, ever timid in Court, easily doused by a robust opponent or an impatient Judge, rose in his seat (once again this is the evidence of Liz Probert) and uttered a furious protest. 'I insist you withdraw that word "shyster".'

'No need for that, Erskine-Brown.' Ballard was being gently judicial. 'Luci is merely talking us through the public perception.'

'You put it, Chair, succinctly and to the point.' Once again, Luci was grateful to the furniture.

'Oh, well. If it's only the public perception.' Erskine-Brown sank back in his seat, apparently mollified.

'What we have to demonstrate is that barristers have outsize hearts. There is no section of the community, and we can prove this by statistics, which cares more deeply, gives more liberally to charity, signs more letters to *The Times*, and shows its concern for the public good by pointing out more frequent defects in the railway system, than the old-fashioned, tried-and-trusted British barrister.'

'You can prove anything by statistics.' Erskine-Brown was still out, in a small way, to cause trouble.

'Exactly so.' Luci seemed unexpectedly delighted. 'So we have chosen our statistics with great care, and we shall use them to the best possible advantage. But I'm not talking statistics here. I'm talking of the situation, sad as I'm sure we all agree it may be, which gives us the opportunity to show that we *do* care.' Luci paused and seemed, for a moment, moved with deep emotion. 'So much so that we should all join in a very public display of heartfelt thanks.'

'Heartfelt thanks for what?' Erskine-Brown was mystified. 'Surely not our legal-aid fees?'

At this point, Luci produced copies of a statement she invited Erskine-Brown to circulate. When Liz Probert got it, she found that it read:

We wish to give heartfelt thanks for the life of one of our number. An ordinary, workaday barrister. An old warhorse. One who didn't profess to legal brilliance, but one who cared deeply and whom we loved as a fellow member of number 4 Equity Court.

'By this act we shall show that barristers have hearts,' Luci summed up the situation.

'By what act is that, exactly?' Erskine-Brown was still far from clear.

'The Memorial Service. In the Temple Church for the late Horace Rumpole, barrister at law. Chair, I'm sure we can rely on you for a few remarks, giving thanks for a life of quiet and devoted service.'

It later emerged that at this stage of the Chambers meeting Liz Probert, undoubtedly the most sensible member of the gathering, suggested that a discussion of a Memorial Service was a little premature in view of the fact that there had as yet been no announcement of Rumpole's death. Erskine-Brown told her that he had spoken to She Who Must Be Obeyed, who was, he said, 'putting a brave face on it', but admitted that I had been removed from the hospital to which I had been rushed after a dramatic failure in the ticker department, brought about by an unusually brutal encounter with Judge Ballingham, to the Primrose Path Home in Sussex, and would not be back in Chambers for a very long time indeed. In that case, Liz suggested, all talk of a Memorial Service might be postponed indefinitely.

'Put our programme on hold?' Luci was clearly disappointed. 'It'd be a pity not to continue with the planning stage. Naturally, Mrs Rumpole's hoping for the best, but let's face it, at his age Rumpole's actuarial chances of survival are approximate to a negative-risk situation –'

'And one knows, doesn't one,' Erskine-Brown asked, 'what places like the Primrose Path are like? They call themselves "Homes", but the reality is they are –'

'What do you think they are?' Liz Probert was cynical enough to ask. 'Houses of ill fame? Gambling dens? Five-star hotels?'

'They are places,' Erskine-Brown was looking at her, she said, more in sorrow than in anger, 'where people are sent to end their days in peace. They call themselves "convalescent homes" to reassure the relatives. But the truth of it is that not many people come out of them alive.'

4

'We'll need to put together a programme.' Ballard was seriously worried. 'And we can hardly ask Mrs Rumpole for her help. As yet.'

'I have an aunt in Godalming.' Erskine-Brown seemed unnaturally proud of the fact. 'I can call in on Rumpole when I go down to see her next.'

'And I'm sure your visit, Erskine-Brown,' Ballard said, 'will be a welcome treat for Rumpole.'

As usual, our Head of Chambers had got it completely wrong.

So now Claude and I were together in my room in the Primrose Path Home, somewhere on the sleepy side of Sussex. It was a place of unremitting cleanliness, and so tidy that I was homesick for the unwashed ashtray, resting place for the butt ends of small cigars, the pile of unreturned briefs, the dusty, yellowing accounts of ancient crimes (for which those found guilty must have now completed their sentences), outdated copies of Archbold on Criminal Law and Procedure, and the Old English Law Reports, bound in crumbling leather and gathering dust, as did the collapsing umbrella left by some long-forgotten client. On the mantelpiece I kept a few souvenirs of my notable cases: the bullet found embedded in the radiogram in the Penge Bungalow affair, the china mug inscribed to a 'Perfect Dad' from which Leonard Peterson had drunk his last, arsenic-flavoured cup of tea, and the sheet music of 'In a Monastery Garden', which Mrs Florence Davenport had been playing as she awaited the news of her husband's death after his brakes had been partially severed by her lover.

By contrast, the Primrose Path Home was uncomfortably tidy. The atmosphere was heavy with the smell of furniture polish, chemical air fresheners and disinfectant. There was a constant hum of hoovering and the staff seemed to handle everything, including the patients, with rubber gloves.

'What's your favourite music, Rumpole?'

'Music, Erskine-Brown?'

'Schubert Trio? Mozart Concerto? We know you're absurdly prejudiced against Wagner. What about "When I was a little page" from Verdi's *Falstaff*?'

'I never was a little page! Don't babble, Erskine-Brown.'

'Or Elgar? Typically English, Elgar.'

'When I sing to myself, which is only very occasionally –' Poor old Claude seemed, for no particular reason, to be in some distress, and I was doing my best to help him out.

'Yes. Yes!' His nose twitched with excitement. 'Tell me, Rumpole. When you sing to yourself, what do you sing?'

'Sometimes "Pop Goes the Weasel". Occasionally "Knock'd 'em in the Old Kent Road". More often than not a ballad of the war years, "We're going to hang out the washing on the Siegfried Line." You remember that, don't you?'

'No, Rumpole, I'm afraid I don't.' Erskine-Brown's nose twitched again, though this time it was a sign of displeasure. He tried another tack. 'Tell me, Rumpole. Talking of the war years, did you ever serve your country overseas?'

'Oh yes,' I told Claude, in answer to his ridiculous question. 'I flew Spitfires in the war. I shot down the Red Baron and was the first British pilot to enter Berlin.'

Claude looked at me sadly and said, 'I only ask because Ballard wants material for his speech.'

'His speech about me?' I was puzzled.

'About your life. To give thanks for your existence.'

It sounded extremely improbable. 'Ballard's going to do that?'

'We shall celebrate you, Rumpole.'

'You mean –' I was hoping against all the probabilities that they were contemplating some sort of party '– a Chambers piss-up in Pommeroy's Wine Bar? Drinks on the Soapy Sam Memorial Fund?'

'Not exactly that, Rumpole.' Claude glanced, nervously I thought, at his watch. 'I'd better be getting back. I've got a rating appeal tomorrow.'

'I envy you, Erskine-Brown. You seem to lead a life of perpetual excitement.'

'Oh, there's just one more thing.' The man was already on his feet. 'Do you have a favourite prayer?'

'Why do you ask?'

'To help us, Rumpole, to celebrate your life.'

'Then I pray to God to be left alone. So I can get out of here as quickly as possible. It's all far too clean for my liking.'

'I'm sure you're quite comfortable here, Rumpole.' Erskine-Brown gave me a smile of faint encouragement. 'And I know they'll look after you extremely well. For as long as you have left.'

At which he stood up and stole silently out of the room with the guilty look of a man leaving a funeral early.

When Erskine-Brown had gone, I watched morning television. A group of people had been assembled, having, it seemed, only one thing in common. They had each had sexual intercourse with someone who turned out to be a close relative. This incident in their lives, which many people might wish to keep discreetly under wraps, led them to speak out at length, as cheerfully as though they were discussing gardening or cookery, to the huge audience of the unemployed, the pensioned-off and the helpless in hospitals. As their eager, confiding faces filled the screen I began to doze off – the best way, I had found, of enjoying life at the Primrose Path Home.

Whoever had christened this place of eternal rest the

Primrose Path betrayed insufficient knowledge of English literature. According to Ophelia in *Hamlet*, it's the path of dalliance – and any dalliance in the home was confined strictly to the television. The porter in *Macbeth*, however, said that the primrose way led 'to the everlasting bonfire'. This may have been a more accurate description. The inhabitants of the rooms down the corridor were given to disappearing quietly during the night and leaving the Primrose Path, I felt sure, for the nearest crematorium.

I woke up, it seemed hours later, to my untouched lunch, a tray mainly loaded with a plethora of paper napkins, much unwelcome salad and a glass of orange juice. I was searching for a mouthful of edible cheese under the stationery when I caught a sound, unusual, even unknown in the Primrose Path. A woman was sobbing. People died there, but you heard no cries of agony, no angry slamming of doors, or wailing of relatives. The sobs I heard were restrained, but they were undeniably heartfelt. I abandoned my lunch, switched off the television and moved, as quietly as I could manage it, into the corridor.

At the end of the passage, with its linoleum shining like polished shoes, a woman was sobbing as she watered a bowl of hyacinths. She was, perhaps, in her late forties, her chestnut hair fading a little, but with high cheekbones, usually amused eyes and a generous mouth. She was Nurse Albright, my favourite member of staff, known to me as Dotty Dorothy, owing to her habit of occasionally promising to dust off my aura by polishing the surrounding air. She also brought me an assortment of roots, herbs and leaves, which, if added to my tea, she promised, would soon make me fit to run a mile, spend a day defending in a murder trial and learn to tango at evening classes. She was, above all, cheerful and unfailingly kind, and we would sing together songs we both loved, songs

I had kept from the prying ears of Erskine-Brown, such as 'Night and Day', 'That Old Black Magic' and 'Bewitched, Bothered and Bewildered', which I had danced to in a far-distant time, before Hilda's and my fox-trotting days were over.

Dotty Dorothy's singing, her use of herbs and strange roots, and, on many occasions, her kindness got her into frequent trouble with her boss, Sister Sheila Bradwell, who ruled the Primrose Path with the kind of enlightened and liberal principles which guided Captain Bligh when he was in charge of the *Bounty*. Sister Sheila recognized no superior being, except for one called Nanki-Poo, an evil-tempered, spoiled and domineering Pekinese whom I had seen the Sister kiss, fondle, feed with chocolate biscuits and generally spoil in a way she would never treat a patient. Like many of the inhabitants of the Primrose Path, Nanki-Poo suffered a degree of incontinence which littered the garden and added some significance to his name. He would also, when out walking, sit down if a leaf attached itself to his trailing hair, and yelp until a nurse came and relieved him of the encumbrance.

It was the sudden appearance of the powerful Sister Sheila, with or without her pet, that Nurse Dotty Albright feared as we stood chatting in the corridor.

'Get back into your room, Mr Rumpole,' Dotty swallowed a sob and wiped an eye on the back of her hand, 'before Sister spots you.'

'Never mind about Sister Sheila.' I had grown impervious to the icy disapproval of the Head Girl. 'Tell me what's the matter.'

'A terrible night, Mr Rumpole. It's been the most ghastly night ever at the Primrose Path.'

'Tell me what happened.'

'Poor Mr Fairweather . . . He passed away during the night.

They took him away. It was my night off and they took him away without even telling me.'

I had caught a glimpse of Fairweather – Freddy, Dotty often called him – a short, beady eyed, bald-headed, broad-shouldered man in a dressing-gown being pushed in a wheel-chair to his room down the corridor. He was recovering, Dotty told me, from a massive heart attack, but she brought him roots and herbal remedies and he made jokes and flirtatious suggestions. Freddy and I, she assured me, were her two favourite patients.

'Can you imagine that?' Dotty said as she took out a crumpled handkerchief and blew her nose gently. 'Sister let them take him without even a chance of saying goodbye. Freddy would have hated that. He was full of rude sugges-tions, of course he was. He was a bit of a jack the lad, we know that, even in his condition of health. But underneath all that, he had the most perfect manners. Even if he'd gone, even if it was too late, he'd have liked me to be there to hold his hand and say goodbye before he passed away. But *she* wouldn't have that. *She* has to know best, always.'

As Dotty went on talking, it appeared that the sad death of Freddy Fairweather wasn't the only disaster of that long, eventful night. A certain Michael Masklyn, high up on the list of unpopular patients, had, in Dotty's words, 'done a runner' and strayed from the Primrose Path under the cover of dark-ness. Masklyn was an unknown quantity; he seemed to have few friends and no visitors except an older woman who had visited him once and, as their voices were raised in a quarrel, was heard to vow never to come near him again. He'd been transferred from a hospital which had, as might be expected, run out of beds, and found a place in the Primrose Path under some sort of government scheme. He had, Dotty assured me, a vile temper, was thankful for nothing, and had once thrown a glass containing his urine sample at the head of a trainee nurse who would do no harm to anybody.

'I never thought he was well enough to get out of here.' Dotty had stopped crying now and her voice was full of anger. 'Sister's security's just hopeless. His clothes were in his room, just as yours are, and Gavin was fast asleep at his desk downstairs. So Mr Masklyn just walked off and left us. I hate to say this to you, Mr Rumpole, but there's just no organization in this place. No organization at all. It's all rules and no practice. Not the place for either of us really, is it?'

Strangely enough, after that sad and eventful evening, the Primrose Path became, in some elusive and quiet way, more interesting. I tried to discuss the break-out of Michael Masklyn with Sister Sheila, but was met with pursed lips and the shortest of possible answers.

'He was an impossible patient,' Sheila Bradwell told me. 'In one way we were glad to get rid of him. But of course we had our duty of care. You can't keep an eye on everyone twenty-four hours a day.'

'Do the police know he's gone missing?' I felt a stirring of the old need to cross-examine the witness.

'We reported it, naturally, Mr Rumpole, if you're so interested. There was no sign of him at his last known address.'

'Did he have a family?'

'Someone he said was his sister came once. No one's been able to track her down either.'

'My friend Dotty says his door was locked in the morning when she came on duty.'

'Your friend Nurse Albright says a lot of things we don't have to take too much notice of. Of course the door wasn't locked at night. We locked it in the morning, until the police came to see if there were any clues to where he'd gone. You don't want the evidence disturbed. You know all about that, don't you, Mr Rumpole?'

'I suppose I do. All the same, it must have been a terrible night for you. I was sorry to hear about Mr Fairweather.'

Sister Sheila Bradwell stood looking at me, a straight-backed, straight-haired woman, born to command. I thought I saw in her eyes not sorrow for the passing of another patient, but a faint amusement at the fact that I had bothered to raise the subject.

'These things happen, Mr Rumpole, at a place like this. They're very sad, but they happen all the time. We've got used to it, of course. And we deal with it as kindly as possible, whatever your friend Nurse Albright may say about the matter.'

'She said she was very fond of Mr Fairweather. He was kind to her, and she enjoyed looking after him.'

'And did your friend tell you that dear old Mr Fairweather had also said he'd left her money in his will?' Sister Bradwell was smiling as she said that, and it came as something of a shock. After being clearly disapproved of for asking imperti-nent questions, it suddenly seemed as though I was being drawn into an argument from which, for the moment, I retreated.

'She never said anything like that. Only that she was upset because he died so suddenly.'

'Well, it's nothing for you to worry about, Mr Rumpole, is it? You can concentrate on getting a good rest. Shall I switch your telly on for you?'

'Please don't.'

'Very well then, Mr Rumpole. And if you take my advice, you'll steer very clear of your friend's herbal remedies. Some of them may have unfortunate results.'

★

In the days that followed, Dotty seemed unusually busy, but late one afternoon, as I woke from a light doze, I found her sitting by my bed with a surprise present. It was half a bottle of claret she had managed to get opened in an off-licence and smuggled in under her mac. We shared a toothglassful of a wine in the same humble class as Château Thames Embankment, but none the less welcome to a palate starved of alcohol. So the old friendly Dotty was back, but quieter and sadder, and I didn't dare suggest even a muted rendition of 'Bewitched, Bothered and Bewildered'.

'They don't want me to go to the funeral,' she said.

'Who doesn't want you to? The family?'

'No, Sister Sheila. And Freddy's special doctor. Freddy wouldn't see anyone else.'

The common run of patients, myself included, were attended to by one of the local GPs. However, the Primrose Path was visited almost daily by a tall, elegantly dressed man in a well-cut suit who moved down the corridor in a deafening smell of aftershave, always escorted by Sister Sheila and referred to by the staff, in tones of considerable awe, as Doctor Lucas.

'I've never got on with that Lucas. Well, they won't even tell me where the funeral's going to be.'

'They won't?'

'They said it was Freddy's special wish. He hated funerals . . .'

'Well, none of us like them. Particularly our own.'

'So he didn't want anyone to be there. That was his last wish, they told me. And, of course, he wanted to be cremated.'

'The primrose way', I thought, 'to the everlasting bonfire'.

'You know what happened? Doctor Lucas and Sister Sheila were with him when he died. They rang the undertaker, they said, and they had him taken away at once. During the night. As though . . . Freddy was something to be ashamed of.'

'You miss him, don't you?'

'Poor old darling. Sometimes he said he was in love.' She put a hand into the pocket of her uniform and pulled out a photograph, a bald-headed, suntanned, bright-eyed elderly man with a nose which looked as though it had, at some distant time in his life, been broken in hostility or sport. He was sitting up in bed, smiling, with his arm round Nurse Dotty. It had been taken, Dotty told me, by trainee Nurse Jones, and they had all been laughing a good deal at the time.

'Sister Sheila said something.' I hesitated before I asked the question. 'Was he going to leave you money in his will?'

'Oh, he told everyone that.' She was smiling now. 'Not that I ever really expected anything, of course. But it just showed how well we got on. He said he didn't have much of a family left to provide for.'

We talked a little more, and she told me that Freddy had a business somewhere in the north of England and he 'wasn't short of a bob or two', and then she asked for my legal advice, adding, 'Do you mind if I pay you with this glass of wine?'

'That makes it as profitable as a conference on Legal Aid,' I told her.

'I'm going to find out about Freddy's funeral. When I've found out, I'm going to it. I don't care what Sister Sheila has to say about it. I'm entitled to do that, aren't I?'

'I'm sure,' I gave her my best legal opinion, 'you're entitled to go to any funeral you choose. I'd even invite you to mine.'

'Don't be silly.' She smiled and, for an unexpected moment of delight, held my hand. 'That's not going to happen. And we're not going to stay here much longer, are we? Either of us. The Primrose Path's really just not our sort of place.'

★

'Not our sort of place.' Dotty's words, together with her account of the ease with which the awkward customer Masklyn had escaped from the Primrose Path, fired my enthusiasm. I waited for a night when Dotty was not only off duty but had gone to stay with her sister in Haywards Heath. I made sure that she couldn't be blamed by the Obergruppen-führer for my having gone missing from the list of inmates. And I wanted to avoid any lengthy argument with the Primrose Path (whose bill had been paid to the end of this month) or my wife Hilda, which might prolong my term of imprisonment.

The clothes I was wearing when my ticker overreacted so dramatically to the strain put upon it by an appearance before the raging Judge Bullingham had come with me to hospital and from there to the Primrose Path. They were hanging in a cupboard in my room, so I was able to change the pyjamas for my regulation uniform of black jacket and waistcoat, a pair of striped trousers supported by braces, a white shirt with detachable collar, and dark socks with, by this time, dusty and unpolished black shoes. I had kept charge of my wallet, which had four ten-pound notes and a travel pass in it, so I was soon prepared for the dash to freedom. I paused only to scribble a note for Dotty, which contained simply my four-line version of an old song:

> The way you feel my pulse
> The way you test my pee
> The memory of much else
> They can't take that away from me.

I wasn't particularly proud of rhyming 'pulse' with 'else', but time was pressing and I had a journey to make. I signed the message 'Love Rumpole', put the dressing-gown back on over my clothes and moved out stealthily towards the staircase.

The gods who look after the elderly trying to escape the

clutches of the medical profession were on my side. That night a poll was being taken on television to decide the Sexiest Footballer of the Year, an event which had aroused far more interest than any recent election. So the television sets were humming in the rooms, and the nurses had withdrawn to their staff room to watch. The desk in the hallway was, more often than not, manned by Gavin, a quiet and serious young man to whom a shaven head and an over-large brown jumper gave a curiously monkish appearance. He was studying somewhere, but turned up for nights at the Primrose Path, where he read until dawn. His attendance was irregular, and, as on the night that Michael Masklyn walked free, he was away from his desk. I slid back bolts, undid chains and passed out into the night.

Somewhere in the back streets of the town I discarded the dressing-gown, tossing it over a hedge into somebody's front garden as a surprise present. I found a spotted bow tie in a jacket pocket and fixed it under my collar. Accoutred as though for the Old Bailey, I presented myself at the railway station, where the last train to Victoria was, happily, half an hour late.

My first call in London was to Equity Court. Our Chambers were silent and empty, the clerks' room was fuller than ever of screens and other mechanical devices and I searched in vain for briefs directed to me. I went into my room, which seemed on first glance to be depressingly tidy. However, the eagle eyes of the tidier-up had missed a half-full packet of small cigars at the back of a drawer. I lit one, puffed out a perfect smoke ring, and then I noticed a glossy little folder, which looked like the advertisement for a country hotel or a tour of the Lake District, except that the cover bore the words 'Equity Court Chambers' with the truncated address 'bestofthebar.com'. There was an unappealing photograph captioned 'Samuel Ballard QC, Chair and Head of Chambers' standing in the doorway as though to tempt in passing trade.

Inside, on the first page, was a list of our Chambers' members. My eye was immediately drawn to one entry, 'Horace Rumpole, BA Oxon', against which someone had written with a felt-tip pen, 'Deceased?'. I immediately lifted the telephone and called my home in Froxbury Mansions.

'Rumpole, is that you?' Hilda sounded as though I had woken her from a deep sleep.

'Yes. It's me, Rumpole. And not Rumpole deceased either. It's Rumpole alive and kicking.'

'Isn't it way past bedtime in the Primrose Path?'

'I don't care what bedtime is in the Primrose Path. I'm not in the Primrose Path any more. I've put the Primrose Path far behind me. I'm in Chambers.'

'You're in Chambers? Whatever are you doing in Chambers? Go back to the nursing home at once!' Hilda's orders were clear and to be disobeyed at my peril. I took the risk.

'Certainly not. I'm coming home to Gloucester Road. And I don't need nursing any more.'

It would be untrue to say that there was – at first, anyway – a hero's welcome for the returning Rumpole. There were no flowers, cheers, or celebratory bottles opened. There was the expected denunciation of the defendant Rumpole as selfish, ungrateful, irresponsible, opinionated, wilful and, not to put too fine a point upon it, a pain in the neck to all who had to deal with him. But behind these stiff sentences, I got the strange and unusual feeling that Hilda was fairly pleased to see me alive and kicking and to discover that I had, so far as could be seen, passed out of the Valley of the Shadow of Death and had come back home, no doubt to give trouble, probably to fail to cooperate with her best-laid schemes, but at least not gone for ever.

I have to admit that our married life has not been altogether plain sailing. There have been many occasions when the icy winds of Hilda's disapproval have blown round Froxbury Mansions. There have been moments when the journey home from the Temple felt like a trip up to the front line during a war which seemed to have no discernible ending. But, in all fairness, I have to say that her behaviour in the matter of the Rumpole Memorial Service was beyond reproach. She told me of the impending visit of the two QCs, and when Ballard let her know, over the telephone, that they planned a 'fitting tribute to Rumpole's life', she guessed what they were after and even suffered, she admitted with apparent surprise, a curious feeling of loss. She had telephoned the Primrose Path and spoken to Sister Sheila, who was able to tell her, much to her relief, that 'Mr Rumpole was being as awkward as ever!' Now that I appeared to be back in the land of the living, she was prepared to fall in with my master plan and enable me to eavesdrop, as the two leading pomposities of our Chambers unfolded their plans to mark the end of Rumpole's life on earth.

Accordingly, I was shut away in the kitchen when Ballard and Erskine-Brown arrived. Hilda left the sitting-room door ajar, and I moved into the hall to enjoy the conversation recorded here.

'We're sure you would like to join us in offering up thanks for the gift of Rumpole's life, Mrs Rumpole,' Soapy Sam started in hushed and respectful tones.

'A gift?' She Who Must Be Obeyed sounded doubtful. 'Not a free gift, certainly. It had to be paid for with a certain amount of irritation.'

'That,' Ballard had to concede, 'is strictly true. But one has to admit that Horace achieved a noticeable position in the Courts. Notwithstanding the fact that he remained a member of the Junior Bar.'

'Albeit a rather elderly member of the Junior Bar,' Claude had to remind Hilda.

'It's true that he never took a silk gown *or* joined us in the front row. The Lord Chancellor never made him a QC,' Ballard admitted.

'His face didn't fit,' Claude put it somewhat brutally, I thought, 'with the establishment.'

'All the same, many of the cases he did brought him –' Ballard hesitated and Claude supplied the word:

'Notoriety.'

'So we want to arrange a Memorial Service. In the Temple Church.'

It was at this point that She Who Must Be Obeyed offered a short, incredulous laugh. 'You mean a Memorial Service for *Rumpole*?'

'That, Mrs Rumpole, Hilda if I may,' Ballard seemed relieved that the conversation had, at last, achieved a certain clarity, 'is exactly what we mean.'

'We're sure that you, of course, Hilda, and Rumpole's family and friends would wish to join us in this act of celebration.'

'Friends?' Hilda sounded doubtful and added, I thought unkindly, 'Rumpole has friends?'

'Some friends, surely. From all sections of society.'

'You mean you're going to invite that terrible tribe of South London criminals?' I thought this ungrateful of Hilda. The Timsons' addiction to ordinary decent crime had kept us in groceries, including huge quantities of furniture polish, washing-up liquid and scouring pads, and had frequently paid the bill at the butcher's and several times redecorated the bathroom over the long years of our married life.

'I hardly think,' Claude hastened to reassure her, 'that the Timsons would fit in with the congregation at the Temple Church.'

'I'm sure there will be many people,' Ballard was smiling at She Who Must, 'who aren't members of the criminal fraternity and who'll want to give Rumpole a really good send-off.'

It was at this point that I entered the room, carrying a bottle of Château Thames Embankment and glasses. 'Thank you for that kind thought, Ballard,' I greeted him. 'And now you're both here, perhaps we will all drink to Rumpole revived.'

Hamlet, happening to bump into his father's ghost on the battlements, couldn't have looked more surprised than my learned friends.

The return to life was slow and, in many ways, painful. At first there was a mere trickle of briefs. Bonny Bernard, my favourite solicitor, had given up hope of my return and sent a common theft charge against two members of the Timson clan to Hoskins in our Chambers. I'm only too well aware of the fact that Hoskins has innumerable daughters to support, but I had to make sure that the Timsons knew I was no longer dead, and had to finance a wife with a passion for cleaning materials, as well as the life-giving properties of Pommeroy's Very Ordinary Claret.

I was sitting in my room in Chambers, wondering if I would ever work again, when our clerk, Henry, put through a phone call and I heard, to my delight, the cheerful voice of Sister Dotty, although on this memorable occasion the cheerfulness seemed forced and with an undertone of deep anxiety. After the usual enquiries about whether or not I was still alive, and the news that she was doing freelance and temporary nursing and had taken a small flat in Kilburn, she said, with a small and unconvincing laugh, 'I had a visit from the police.'

'You had a burglary?'

'No. They wanted me to help them with their enquiries.'

I felt a chill wind blowing. People who help the police with their enquiries often end up in serious trouble.

'Enquiries about what?'

'Poor old Freddy Fairweather's death. They suggest I call in at the station and bring my solicitor. And I haven't really got a solicitor.'

'Then I'll get you one. Where are you? I'll ring you back.'

This was clearly a job for my old friend Bonny Bernard. I called him to remind him that I was, in spite of all the evidence to the contrary, up for work, and put him in touch with Dotty. A few days later, they called in at my Chambers to report the result of an extraordinary conversation which had taken place with Detective Inspector Maundy and Detective Sergeant Thorndike in a nick not too far from the Primrose Path Home.

'They were a decent enough couple of officers,' Bernard told me. 'But they soon made their suspicions clear to me and the client.'

'Suspicions of what?'

'Murder.'

I looked at Dotty, all her smiles gone to be replaced with a bewildered, incredulous terror. I did my best to make light of the moment. 'You haven't done in Sister Sheila?'

'They're investigating the death of one of the patients,' Bernard said. 'A Mr Frederick Fairweather.'

'Freddy! As though I'd do anything to hurt him. We were friends. You know that. Just as we were, Mr Rumpole.'

'And what's she supposed to have done to Fairweather?'

'Digitalis.' Bernard looked at his notes.

'Foxgloves?' I remembered Dotty's collection of herbal remedies.

'It's used to stabilize the action of the heart.' Words began to pour out of Dotty. 'They asked me about the access I had to digitalis, they seemed to think that I had a huge collection of pills and potions . . .'

'Well, you had, hadn't you?'

'Herbal remedies, you know that. And, of course, I had digitalis, but I'd enter every dose I had to give a patient – and I never treated Freddy with it at all.'

'So what do they suggest?' I asked Bernard.

'That they have evidence my client used a whole lot of digitalis without entering it or keeping a note,' he told me. 'And that she was seen coming out of Fairweather's room an hour before he died. She also boasted she was going to benefit from the deceased's will.'

'It's all completely ridiculous!' Dotty could contain herself no longer. 'I went to bed early and never left my room until I went on duty next day. I didn't care a scrap about Freddy's will. I only wanted him to get better, that was all I wanted. Nothing would have made me harm him, nothing in the world!'

She was crying, I remembered, as she watered a bowl of hyacinths after Freddy Fairweather died. She was crying again now, but angrily, dabbing at her eyes with the clutched ball of a handkerchief.

'That Doctor. Lucas, was it? He must have entered the cause of death?' I asked Bernard.

'The cause of death was a heart attack. The deceased had heart problems. But Lucas told the Inspector that what he saw might also have been brought about by an overdose of digitalis.'

I made a note and then asked Dotty, 'You told me you were going to Freddy's cremation. Did you go?'

'It was very strange. I rang the undertakers that used to come to the Primrose Path, but they knew nothing about Freddy. Then I rang the crematorium and I got a date. It was terrible, Mr Rumpole, just terrible. There was no one there. Absolutely no one at all. Sheila had said Freddy didn't want anyone to see him go, but I couldn't believe it. I was alone, in that horrible place . . . I think they were waiting for someone to come. I don't know who they thought I was. One of the family, even a wife, perhaps. I told them I was his nurse and they said they might as well begin. There was some sort of music. I suppose they had it left over from someone else's funeral, but there was no one to say anything. Not a word. Not a prayer. And there was just me to watch the coffin slide away behind the curtains. Apart from me – he went quite alone.' She dabbed her eyes again and then looked up at me. A look full of unanswered questions.

'Did you tell the police that?'

'No. I just answered their questions.'

'And is there anything else you want to tell me?'

'Only that I'm angry. So angry.'

'Because you know who's been talking to the police?'

'Of course. Sister Sheila!'

'You think it's Sheila?'

'Who else could it be?'

'They told us, Mr Rumpole,' Bonny Bernard, of course, had no experience of the mysteries of the Primrose Path Home, 'that they'd be making further enquiries. Of course, we don't know what they'll find out.'

'Perhaps they'll find out,' I told my client Dotty, 'why Sister Sheila should have gone to them with a story like that.'

*

I was, of course, torn. I believed that Nurse Dotty was wholly innocent and would remain innocent even if proven guilty. Nothing would give me greater pleasure than pricking this bubble of so-called evidence and unworthy suspicion, and teaching the Jury to love Nurse Dotty as much as they doubted the thin-lipped and hard-faced Sister who had given evidence for the prosecution. And yet, the more I thought about it, the more there seemed something unconvincing about the whole story, from the escape of the man Masklyn to the tenuous accusation about an overdose of digitalis. The trial, if there was to be a trial, might answer none of these questions. Well, that was often the case with trials. And I needed a sensational case at the Old Bailey, didn't I, to resurrect Rumpole's fading career? Then I felt a pang of guilt. Did I want Dotty to suffer just so that I could, after all these years, do something almost as sensational in court as the case of the Penge Bungalow murders? The 'Primrose Path Crime' would be sure to hit the headlines.

It was while I was turning these matters over in my mind that my room was invaded by a pungent but not unpleasant perfume, and a tall, blonde woman in a black trouser suit came with it. She spoke in a surprisingly deep voice with more than a hint of a Yorkshire accent.

'Got a minute? It's about time we had a word. I'm Luci Gribble. Luci with an "i". I'm your new Director of Marketing and Administration. Sorry I haven't had a window before.'

A window? What was the woman talking about? Was she shut in some airless oubliette in the Chambers cellarage? By now she had made herself comfortable in my clients' chair.

'I never had an *old* Director of Marketing,' I had to tell her. 'So I don't know why I should need a new one.' I had, of course, heard complaints from our clerk, Henry, who regarded Luci with deep suspicion as one likely to butt into his drinks with solicitors and seriously deplete his clerk's fees.

'I'm here to look after your image,' Luci told me.

'I know what that means.' I'd heard it all before. 'It means you think I should get a new hat.'

'Not at all! The hat's perfect! And the striped pants, and the cigar ash down the waistcoat. They all suit your image perfectly. Don't change a thing!'

I suppose I should have found that reassuring, but somehow I didn't.

'I believe,' I told her, 'you were behind the idea of a church service to celebrate my death.'

'To celebrate your life, Horace. That's what we were going to celebrate. Of course, that's on hold. For the time being.'

'I'm glad to hear it.'

'I understand you're going through a bit of a sticky period, practice wise.'

'Sticky?'

'Bit of a lull? A serious shortfall in briefs?'

'Not at all.' I had on my desk the instructions Bonny Bernard had sent me in the matter of Nurse Dotty and I fingered the papers proudly. 'I've just been instructed in a rather sensational murder case.'

'Really?' Luci showed a polite interest. 'Who got murdered?'

'Probably no one. My client's a nurse. It's suggested she murdered a patient called Freddy Fairweather in the Primrose Path Home. A place,' I had to add, 'from which I was extremely glad to escape.'

What Luci said then astonished me. She only seemed mildly surprised. 'Not Freddy Fairweather of Primrose?'

'The Primrose *Path*,' I reminded her.

'I don't know anything about the "Path". The Freddy Fairweather I worked for was Primrose Personal Pensions. He was an IFA – Independent Financial Adviser. Invested anyone's money in what he called a "gilt-edged pension scheme". On the whole, about as gilt-edged as a bouncing cheque. Which is why we parted company. Do you say he's dead?'

'I'm afraid so, and without a memorial service. If he's the same Freddy Fairweather, of course.'

'Short, square shoulders? No hair and a broken nose? He could turn on the charm, Freddy could. Had a bit of a chip on his shoulder as he'd left school at fifteen and never been to university like the rest of the Chamber of Commerce. Of course, if he's been murdered, you never met him, did you, Horace?'

'I might have done, strangely enough. You say you worked for him. Where exactly?'

'You know Leeds, Horace?'

'I'm afraid I have only a sketchy knowledge of Leeds.'

'That's where I started in marketing. I was marketing for Freddy. I won't say they were the best days of my life. I left because I didn't like the way the place was run. And I couldn't stand the company doctor, a quack who was meant to examine the pensioners. Objectionable's not the word.'

'His name wasn't Lucas, was it?'

'Sydney Lucas! That was him! But as for Freddy, he might have cut a few business corners but I wouldn't have wanted to see him murdered.'

I looked at her then, her black-trousered legs crossed, shiny boots pointed, an alien being in the dusty world of Equity Court. I lit a small cigar and, rather to my surprise, she made no protest. I blew out smoke and said, 'I'd be very much obliged if you'd tell me everything you know about the late Freddy Fairweather.'

'All right then. But would you mind passing me one of those whiffs?'

I did so, and we sat smoking and talking together, and what the new Director of Marketing told me was of considerable interest.

It was time to call in old favours. I had entered Pommeroy's Wine Bar in order to arrange overdraft facilities until the Legal Aid cheques came dribbling in (my recuperation at the Primrose Path had not only provided the tempting possibility of a brief in a sensational murder case, but exhausted a cashed-in insurance policy). I stood at the bar waiting for a lugubrious figure, who wore, however pleasant the weather, an elderly mackintosh and the expression of a man suffering from a cold who forever feels a drip forming at the end of his nose. This was, of course, the invaluable sleuth Ferdinand Ian Gilmour Newton, known throughout the legal profession as Fig, who, since adultery no longer had any legal significance, had taken to crime, in which field his investigations were often more thorough, and far more useful, than those carried out by the police.

'Hello, Mr Rumpole.' There was no hint of welcome in Fig's voice; his emotions were hidden under his perpetual raincoat. 'I heard you passed over.'

'I've come back to haunt you, Fig. And also to remind you of the interesting and profitable work I've put your way over many years.'

'Interesting, Mr Rumpole. Rather less profitable. I wouldn't say any of them paid out above the average. What've you got in mind?'

I invested in a bottle of Château Thames Embankment (I'm afraid it was of an indifferent year and not long enough in bottle) and sat Fig down at a quiet table in the corner of the bar. Then I told him all I knew, and all Luci the Marketing Director had told me, about Freddy Fairweather and the

Primrose Path, which had led, in his case so suddenly, 'to the everlasting bonfire'. Then I gave him the list I'd made of all the required information. Fig looked at it doubtfully, like a man invited to swallow peculiarly nasty medicine.

'Are you suggesting, Mr Rumpole, that I do all this as some sort of favour?'

'We'll try and meet your reasonable expenses. I can't promise you much more at the moment.'

There's no point in recording that Fig looked disappointed, his expression was one of perpetual disappointment, but it's enough to say that he didn't jump at my offer.

'Time's money, Mr Rumpole. If you can give me one good reason –'

'All right, Fig,' I said, 'I'll give you a good reason. I'm just back from a near-death experience. Business is slow, not to say boring. An excellent, charming and entirely innocent woman has been accused of a murder. It may all come to nothing, in a way I hope so, but meanwhile the case is shrouded in mystery and I need your help. And if I can't solve it I might as well turn up my toes and hang up my wig.'

It was a long speech, but heartfelt. As I refreshed myself with a gulp of Pommeroy's Very Ordinary I saw something suspiciously like a smile pass over Fig's far-from-cheerful face.

'Don't do that, Mr Rumpole,' he said. 'When do we start?'

I also had more work for Bonny Bernard. After I had reminded him of at least three considerable victories which we had achieved together in the Ludgate Circus Palais de Justice, I was able to persuade him to pursue enquiries at Somerset House and, through a local firm, in the Leeds area, the costs of which might be attributed to Dotty's Legal Aid if her trial ever occurred. I also got him to agree to open informal discussions with that apparently decent and reasonable officer, Detective Inspector Maundy of the Sussex Police.

So south and north my messengers set forth in search of information, and I had nothing much to do but sit in my room awaiting results. I was busily engaged in lighting a small cigar while wrestling with *The Times* crossword puzzle when my phone rang and I heard the voice of Dotty, still troubled, but a little calmer than when I had last seen her. No, she hadn't been summoned to another interview with the forces of law and order. She had, however, had a call from the Primrose Path.

'You heard from Sister Sheila?'

'No. From Gavin. You remember Gavin? The quiet boy, university student. He used to be on the desk at nights. Always had his head in a book.'

'Or else he wasn't there much. He wasn't on guard to prevent the escape of Michael Masklyn. Or, come to that, mine.'

'We used to get on rather well. He seemed a lonely sort of boy. We used to make coffee and talk when I was on nights and nothing much was happening. We argued about God and sex and fidelity and Eminem. All those things that students talk about. It made me feel quite young again. I think he liked me.'

'I'm not at all surprised. Did you talk about the night they took away Freddy Fairweather?'

'He told me, long ago, he was away on some sort of course when that happened. No. This call was about his degree. He's due to get it soon from the University of North Sussex. He asked me to go and watch. I was rather flattered.'

'What's he qualified in? Golf-Course Management? Window Dressing? Spiritual Furniture Arrangement? Aren't they the sort of things you get degrees in nowadays?' I may have sounded cynical; I hadn't yet become fully reconciled to the world I had returned to.

'Nothing like that. Theology.'

I was thinking hard then, about the Primrose Path and young Gavin, occasionally present at the desk downstairs, doing his best to discover how to justify the ways of God to Man. I had advice for Dotty.

'Then I think you should go to the degree ceremony. Definitely. Get a good seat and keep your eyes open.'

And at long last I was ready to return along the Primrose Path. It was an afternoon in early spring, with the trees covered in a green mist of young shoots and pale sunshine on the garden of the home, where a patient or two had been pushed out in wheelchairs to snooze away the few afternoons that were left to them. The front door was open and I stepped into the familiar smell of furniture polish, disinfectant and an air freshener in which the scent of early flowers and budding leaves had been strongly sterilized. I thought, again, how easy it was to get in and out of the Primrose Path without attracting any particular attention. I stood for a minute alone in the hallway, thinking about the eventful night which had led to Dotty's tears, and then a young nurse, one I had not seen before, asked my name and said that Sister Sheila was expecting me in her office.

She didn't move from behind her desk when I came in and her face was set in a frown of stern disapproval, her lips closed as tight as tweezers, so I felt as though I had absconded from some place of conviction and been brought back under escort to face the consequences. Nanki-Poo, a hairy heap in his basket, slept through most of our interview, only occasionally opening an eye and uttering a small snort of disapproval.

'I suppose you've come to apologize for the way you left

us, slinking away like a thief in the night. It merely goes to show that you are still seriously unwell, Mr Rumpole. By the way, there is a bill for extras which you left unpaid.'

I was sitting in a chair opposite her, my hat on the floor, as she pushed a piece of paper towards me.

'I haven't come here to apologize, exactly. I've come here to discuss one of your patients. Frederick Fairweather.'

She gave a short sigh, a quick formal acknowledgement of another death at the Primrose Path. 'Mr Fairweather sadly died, Mr Rumpole, as I believe you know. He had trouble with his heart, as you have. Now, is there anything else you want to say to me?'

So that was her evidence in chief and, as in a courtroom, I was about to cross-examine the witness. I felt a stir of the old excitement, setting out on a series of questions which just might, possibly, expose the truth. I wasn't in Court, of course, and what I was about to do was calculated only to avoid the trial of Dotty on the unsubstantial charge against her. Greater love, I thought, has no man than this, that he give up a defence brief at the Old Bailey for a friend.

'I wonder if you could help me. There are a few little things I'd like to ask about Freddy.' The art of cross-examining, I have always believed, is not the art of examining crossly, and I started in my politest, gentlest and most respectful tone of voice. Lull the witness into a false sense of security was my way, and ask questions she has to agree to before you spring the surprises. 'Mr Fairweather had a company selling private pensions up in Leeds, hadn't he?'

'That was his business, was it? Then you know more than I do.' Sheila was expressionless, and now Nanki-Poo snorted.

'Oh, I doubt that. And his business was called Primrose Personal Pensions, wasn't it? And this is the Primrose Path Home.'

'A pure coincidence.' Sister Sheila was, for the first time, on the defensive.

'Really? There are a lot of coincidences, aren't there, about that eventful night? But let's stick to his business for a moment. Didn't he buy this home as an investment about ten years ago? That was when you'd started to run it, and you got to know him rather well. Isn't that the truth of the matter?'

'I really don't see why I should sit here answering questions about the home's private business. That is absolutely no concern of yours, Mr Rumpole.'

'I'm afraid it *is* my business, Mrs Fairweather.'

There was a silence then. A heavy stillness, during which the dog made no sound and Sister Sheila moved not at all. She sat looking at her undrunk cup of coffee, and the plate on which four chocolate biscuits lay in a neat pattern. Then she managed to whisper, 'What did you call me?'

'By your name. You married Freddy last year, didn't you, at a Leeds Register Office? He was the divorced husband of Barbara Elizabeth Threadwell, by whom he had one son, Gavin. A quiet boy who got into university to read theology and is occasionally on duty at the desk in the hallway. I suppose you got Freddy to marry you as part of the deal.'

'Deal?' The witness was now making the mistake of asking *me* questions. 'What sort of a deal are you suggesting?'

So I told her. 'Primrose Personal Pensions is in serious trouble, isn't it? The pensions just aren't there any more. The poor devils who subscribed to Primrose have no comfortable income to look forward to. God knows what'll happen to them. They'll be sleeping in doorways and dying on the National Health because the truth of the matter is that Freddy trousered their money. Then he had nowhere to hide, except a quiet nursing home run by his wife, where he could be treated by his company doctor, who would issue endless chits assuring the world and the Fraud Squad that Freddy was far too ill to come to Court.

Had I been advising Sister Sheila at that moment, she would have refused to answer further questions on the grounds that they might incriminate her. Without the advantages of my advice, she tried to discover the strength of the evidence against her.

'Mr Rumpole, are you telling me you knew Mr Fairweather well?'

'Since I left here I've got to know him very well indeed.'

'You must be seriously ill, Mr Rumpole.' A faint smile appeared on Sister Sheila's face, a smile of derision. 'Since you left here Mr Fairweather has, as you well know, been dead.'

'Are you sure?'

'Sure?' She spoke as though there was no possible doubt about the matter. 'Of course I'm sure.'

'It would have been what he wanted.' I seemed to surprise her.

'You think he wanted to die?' The smile was overtaken by a brief, mirthless laugh. 'People who come here don't *want* to die, Mr Rumpole.'

'Not everyone has the Fraud Squad and the Pensions Watchdog breathing down their necks. Not everyone has filched thousands of pensioners' money. The time was coming when Dr Lucas's chits and Freddy's shelter in the Primrose Path might not have been enough. There was only one place left for him to hide in. Death.'

'Are you suggesting my patient committed suicide?'

'Of course not. Freddy wouldn't give up as easily as that. His way out, and I think you know this as well as I do, was a death which was as much a fake as his pensions.'

'That's a most outrageous suggestion!' Sister Sheila, as so

many witnesses do when they strike a sticky patch, fell back on righteous indignation. 'My lawyers will make sure you pay for it. And never repeat it.'

'Oh, I think your lawyers will have more important business on their hands. I'm sure Freddy's death was discussed, but not planned exactly. No one could have planned the great opportunity of that night. It was more by luck, wasn't it, than good management?'

'Mr Rumpole,' Sister Sheila gave a magnificent display of patience with a questioner in an advanced stage of senile decay, 'Mr Fairweather died of heart failure. Confirmed by Doctor Lucas. His body was cremated, an event which was witnessed by your friend, Nurse Albright, who says he promised her something in his will.'

'Let me first deal with that.' I fed her tightly controlled fury by smiling tolerantly as I counted off the points on my fingers. 'Doctor Lucas had spent years as the official medical adviser to a fraudulent pension company. Like you, I'm sure he expected to share in the spoils. You did your best to keep the date and place of Freddy's funeral a secret, but Dotty made her own enquiries. It's true she saw a coffin slide into the everlasting bonfire, but whose coffin was it, exactly?'

'Freddy's, of course.' By now the witness was standing, furious, all pretence that we were just discussing another unfortunate patient gone. 'Who else could it have been?'

'A man called Masklyn?' I suggested. 'A transfer from a crowded hospital. A man no one knew much about. No apparent friends. No traceable relatives. He left the hospital that night. Was it, perhaps, the night *he* happened to die? I'm not saying you and Lucas killed him. I don't think you did, I just think his death was a stroke of luck. It meant that one of you could tell the undertaker that the dead man's name was Frederick Fairweather.

'And now, do you want to know why I've gone to the trouble of finding all this out? Because you got in a panic when you thought Dotty was asking too many questions and finding out too much about that dubious event in the crematorium. So what did you do? You decided Dotty would lose her credibility if she was a murder suspect and not a reliable witness. So you spun the police some ridiculous story about too much digitalis, as though she would have killed Freddy because he'd promised to remember her in his will! I'm sure he liked her. But there wasn't any will, any more than there was any fatal heart attack. When you next see Freddy, give him my regards and ask him if he's enjoying his death.'

I got up to go then, and the room, which had seemed so still, was suddenly full of movement. Nanki-Poo jumped out of his basket and started to bark, a high-pitched, irritable yelp like a particularly difficult patient complaining hysterically. At the same time, the door opened and Doctor Sydney Lucas stood in my way. He was looking at me in what I took to be a distinctly unfriendly fashion.

'He's mad!' I heard Sister Sheila tell him. 'He's come back to us and he's seriously insane. He's been talking nonsense to me about poor Freddy.'

Doctor Lucas filled the doorway, considerably younger, taller and a great deal stronger than I am.

'Excuse me' was all I could think of to say. 'Detective Inspector Maundy of the local Force is waiting for me outside. He'll be very worried if I don't emerge. I did warn him that I might have some difficulty leaving . . .'

Whatever they had done to help a crooked businessman disappear from the face of the earth, however outrageous and reckless that plan had been, and however dishonest the doctor's conduct, the mention of the local constabulary made

35

him step away from the door. I walked past him and out into air no longer freshened by chemicals. A cloud had covered the sun, there was a stirring of wind and I felt heavy drops of rain. Wheelchairs were being hurriedly pushed into shelter. I walked away from the Primrose Path for the last time and towards the forces of law and order. I was prepared to make a statement.

The University of North Sussex is not an old foundation. The main hall is a modern glass and concrete building, in front of which stands a large piece of abstract statuary built, so far as I could see, of flattened and twisted girders and bits and pieces of motionless machinery. But inside the steeply raked amphitheatre the Chancellor, professors and lecturers were decked out in pink and scarlet gowns with slung-back mediaeval hoods.

I sat with Dotty among the parents, behind the rows of students. A cleric in a purple gown, the head of the theology department, was calling out names, and the Chairman of the local waste-disposal company, earlier granted an Honorary Doctorate of Literature, handed out the scrolls. Gavin, in his clean white shirt and rarely worn suit, looked younger than ever, hardly more than a schoolboy. As he waited his turn in the queue, his eyes were searching the audience. When he saw Dotty he gave her a small, grateful wave and a smile. Then his name was called and he stepped forward.

'Look now,' I gave Dotty an urgent instruction. 'Look at the entrances.'

She turned and I turned with her. High above us, at the top of the raked seats, there were three doorways. He was standing in the middle one. He must have just moved to where he could see his son, far below him, get his degree. He stood there, a small, broad-shouldered, square figure with a broken nose. It was a moment of pride he had not been able to resist and, as a great chancer, why shouldn't he have taken this risk to see Gavin get what he had never had – a university degree? Gavin shook hands with the waste-disposal magnate and went off with his scroll. Freddy Fairweather turned away, meaning to disappear again into the world of the dead. But he was stopped by Fig Newton and DS Thorndike, who had been waiting for him at my suggestion.

So the case of the Primrose Path never got me a brief. Neither Sister Sheila nor Doctor Sydney Lucas, when arraigned for their various offences, thought of employing Rumpole to defend them. Freddy Fairweather ended up in an open prison, from which he may expect an early release owing to the unexpected onset of Alzheimer's disease. Gavin has taken Holy Orders and returned to Leeds. I still meet Dotty, from time to time, for tea in the Waldorf Hotel, where we sing, quietly but with pleasure, the old standards together.

The day after Freddy Fairweather was arrested, Henry brought a brief into my room. 'Good news at last, Mr Rumpole,' he said. '*R. v. Denis Timson*. Receiving stolen DVDs. It should be interesting. You won't get cases like that from our so-called Marketing Director.' But I have to say, it was to the Marketing Director I owed my greatest debt of gratitude when I came back to the land of the living and solved the mystery of the Primrose Path Home.

Rumpole and the
New Year's Resolutions

'Offer her your seat, Rumpole.' These were the instructions of my wife Hilda, known to me only as She Who Must Be Obeyed. 'Have you forgotten your New Year's resolution?'

'It's only New Year's Eve,' I complained. We were on a crowded tube train on our way south of the river. 'The resolutions don't come into force until tomorrow.' I was rather fond of my seat. Seats were in short supply and I had laid claim to mine as soon as we got on.

'You'd better start now and get into practice. Go over and offer that woman your seat.'

The woman in question seemed to be surrounded by as many children as the one who lived in a shoe. There were perhaps a dozen or more, scattered about the carriage, laughing, shouting, quarrelling, reluctantly sharing sweets, bombarding her for more as she hung to a strap. They were of assorted sexes and colours, mainly in the ten-to-thirteen-year-old bracket. I thought she might have been a schoolteacher taking them to some improving play or concert. But as I approached her I got a whiff of a perfume that seemed, even to my untutored nose, an expensive luxury for a schoolteacher. Another noticeable thing about her was a white lock, a straight line like a dove's feather across black hair. She was also, and I thought this unusual, wearing gloves of a colour to match her suit.

'Excuse me.' The train had picked up speed and gave a sudden lurch which, although I had my feet planted firmly apart, almost toppled me. I put out a hand and grabbed an arm clothed in soft velvet.

The woman was engaged in urgent conversation with a small boy, who, while asking her whether they were getting out at the next station, seemed to be offering her something, perhaps some sort of note or message, which she took from him with a smile. Then she turned to me with an expression of amused concern. 'I say,' she said, 'are you all right?'

'I'm not doing badly,' I reassured her, 'but I just wanted to make sure *you* were all right.'

'Yes, of course I am. But shouldn't you sit down?'

'No, no.' I felt the situation sliding out of control. 'Shouldn't *you* sit down?' Her smile was about to turn into laughter. 'I've come to offer you my seat.'

'Please don't! Why don't you go back and sit on it? Your need is obviously far greater than mine. Anyway, we're all getting out at the Oval.'

It was an embarrassing moment. I knew how Saint George might have felt if, when he was about to release the beautiful princess, she'd told him to go home and that she was far happier tied up to a tree with the dragon.

'Your first gentlemanly act, Rumpole,' Hilda was unforgiving when I returned to my seat, 'and you couldn't pull it off.'

We climbed up from the bowels of the earth into the moderately fresh air of fashionable Kennington. The street was full on New Year's Eve, crowded with faces lit by the strip lights in front of betting shops and pizza parlours. Collars were turned up and hands deep in pockets on a cold end to the year during which I had undergone a near-death experience. This had led to my return to Chambers and solving – a certain sign that a full complement of marbles had been returned to me – the complicated mystery of the Primrose Path.

At the corner of the street, where Luci Gribble, the Chambers' new Director of Marketing and Administration, was giving the New Year's Eve party to which we had been invited, I saw, in a dark doorway, somebody sleeping. This in itself was no surprise. In enough London doorways tattered sleeping bags were being unrolled, newspapers folded in for extra cover, as the occupying army of the homeless camped for the night. But in this particular doorway a large dog was curled up and, embracing it, as though for warmth, was a pale-faced boy, about twelve years old.

Of course I stopped, of course I told Hilda we should do something. But, again of course, like all the passers-by on that cold New Year's evening, we did nothing.

'We don't know the full story, Rumpole.' She Who Must was happily free from doubt. 'He's probably with someone. Perhaps they're coming back for him.'

'Coming back from where?' I asked her.

'I'm sure I don't know. How can we know the whole history of everyone who's sheltering in a doorway? Now, are we going to this party we've come all this way for, or aren't we?'

I don't blame Hilda in the least for this. I blame myself for going on, down the dark street of small, Victorian houses, to Luci's party, while the picture of the pale boy sleeping curled round a stray dog was left hanging in my mind.

It was still there when I stood leaning against the wall in Luci Gribble's flat, trying to balance a glass of Carafino red on a plate of cold cuts and potato salad and doing my best to eat and drink. I was in a room from which most of the seating had been removed, to be replaced by as many of our Marketing and Administration Director's close personal friends as might have filled up the Black Hole of Calcutta.

'I was just looking for a seat,' I appealed to Luci as she loomed up from the throng. She came resplendent in some sort of luminous jacket, and her surprisingly deep voice was cut across, as always, by the fresh breeze of a Yorkshire accent.

'I don't want people sitting down, Rumpole,' she told me. 'I want them standing up, so they can meet each other, form new relationships and network. I asked our Chair,' she looked round at the sea of chattering, chomping and eagerly swilling faces, 'but he hasn't come.' By 'Chair' I suspected she meant our Head of Chambers, Soapy Sam Ballard. 'I don't expect his wife wanted to let him out, even though it is New Year's Eve.'

Soapy Sam had married the matron at the Old Bailey, a determined woman who, after long years of handing out Elastoplasts to defendants who had bumped their heads against cell walls and Aspirin tablets to barristers with piercing headaches brought about by acute anxiety and too many bottles of Pommeroy's plonk, had retired from the dispensary.

'You brought *your* wife, didn't you, Horace? I expect she's more tolerant and broad-minded than Sam's, isn't she?'

I was still doing my best to apply the adjectives 'tolerant' and 'broad-minded' to She Who Must Be Obeyed when Luci gave me another culture shock.

'No doubt Sam's wife keeps him on a pretty short lead. After all, he is extremely attractive physically, isn't he?'

Luci might be, I thought, a wizard at Marketing and Administration, but her powers of observation seemed, in this instance, somewhat flawed. 'You're speaking, are you,' I checked carefully, 'of Samuel Ballard, QC, leading light of the Lawyers as Christians Society? The man who is seriously concerned at the number of teaspoons of instant coffee our junior clerk uses per cup?'

'It's that little-boy look, Horace. It makes you want to hug him, doesn't it?'

I was about to tell Luci that I had never, at any time, felt the slightest temptation to hug Soapy Sam Ballard, when a grey-haired man with a gentle voice didn't so much approach us as was washed up against us by the moving tide of Luci's guests.

'I want you to meet Derek Ridgley, Director of UA. He so much wants to meet you, Horace,' Luci introduced.

'Luci's told me you have a store of legal anecdotes, Mr Rumpole. Have you?'

What was I expected to do, balance my supper and glass of wine while reciting golden oldies from the life of an Old Bailey hack? 'I might have a few,' I told the man cautiously.

'I wondered if you'd speak to us at a fund-raising dinner for UA. Urchins Anonymous, Mr Rumpole. We're concerned about homeless children in London.' As he spoke, I seemed to see again the boy asleep in the doorway, hugging a dog for warmth. 'You wouldn't believe how many children are still sleeping on the streets. Ignorance and Want. You remember the children Dickens wrote about? It's changed far less than you might think. Only last night we found a ten-year-old girl who'd been sleeping for a month on the steps of a church. Luci used to help us with our PR. She suggested you might speak at our dinner.'

I'd left a child asleep on the street and all I could do about it was to tell jokes at a charity do. Speaking at a dinner seemed an inadequate reaction, but, I supposed, better than nothing. 'Of course I will.'

'Good man! It's a great organization, UA. I've worked for it since I came out of the navy. We rely so much on voluntary helpers.'

And then the chimes of midnight rang out from the telly in

a corner of the room. I crossed my arms and my hands were grasped by Luci and the man from Urchins Anonymous and we swayed to the tune of Auld Lang Syne.

It was New Year's Day when Hilda and I emerged into the street. The boy and the dog had disappeared from the doorway to be replaced by a man in a bobble hat, wrapped in a grey blanket. He lit a cigarette as we passed and I saw his face. He was smiling at me as though he was unexpectedly happy or very drunk.

New Year's Day dawned bright and frosty over the Gloucester Road. Remembering Hilda's icy disapproval when I turn up late for breakfast, I pulled on my warm dressing-gown, ran a comb through what was left of my hair, blew my nose and presented myself in the kitchen full of apologies.

'Must have overslept,' I told Hilda. 'Don't know how it could've happened.'

To my amazement, what I was looking at was a sympathetic smile on the face of She Who Must Be Obeyed. Instead of the sharp wind of a rebuke from my life partner, she was purring, like a cat who has just been handed a saucer full of cream.

'It's good for you to sleep, Rumpole. You need the rest. You work so hard. I'm amazed at how you keep going.'

Not half as amazed as I was by this extraordinary change of character, was what I didn't say.

'Now what would you like for breakfast?'

'Just a cup of coffee. If you've got one made.'

I should point out that Hilda, apparently anxious about the Rumpole girth (a fact of nature that has never troubled me in the least), had insisted lately that I take nothing but a plate of muesli (even though I dislike the taste of dried cardboard) and carrot juice for breakfast – a meal which caused me to rush off to the Tastee Bite, a greasy spoon in Fleet Street, for an emergency cholesterol replacement.

Now she made a surprising offer. 'What can I cook you? Bacon? A couple of sausages? Two eggs sunny side up on a fried slice? We might have some potatoes . . .'

By now I was getting anxious. 'Hilda, are you feeling quite well?'

'Not altogether well, Rumpole. Hurt. Deeply hurt.'

'I'm sorry?'

'I've had a letter from Dodo Mackintosh.' The hand with which she lifted the sheet of notepaper from the table was, I thought, trembling. Dodo was one of her oldest friends, both having survived the tough experience of Saint Elfreda's Boarding School for Girls. 'You don't think I'm bossy, do you, Rumpole?'

For once in my long life at the Bar, I was stuck for a reply. I could only mutter, 'Bossy? Of course not! Perish the thought!'

'Dodo tells me I am.'

I gave, I thought, a convincing imitation of a man who has just been told that the world is, contrary to all previously held beliefs, flat. 'Why ever should your old friend Dodo Mackintosh say such a thing?'

'I really don't know,' Hilda sighed. 'I merely wrote and told her I thought her new living-room curtains were a horrible mistake, and that she should really find a more interesting subject for her watercolours than Lamorna Cove in the rain. Oh, and I probably reminded her that to go shopping in a T-shirt and jeans, topped with a baseball hat, at her age was simply to invite ridicule.'

'Might you,' I hazarded a guess, 'have added something about mutton dressed as lamb?'

'I possibly said something to that effect. But, Rumpole,'

she looked at me in what I took to be an appealing fashion, 'I have made a New Year's resolution.' At this point, Hilda stood and spoke as though she were swearing an oath of allegiance to some great cause. 'I shall never be bossy again. I shall do my very best,' I couldn't believe my ears, but she said this, 'to respect the wishes of others. Including you.'

She then cooked my fry-up and a great change seemed to have come over the world.

Hilda's resolution survived, and the change was decidedly marked, as the year stretched, yawned, staggered to its feet and began to set off on the same old search for briefs and moments of relaxation after Court in Pommeroy's. Soapy Sam Ballard was full of his own importance, being widely reported in the tabloids for the prosecution of a stalker who had bombarded Jenny Turnbull, the famous television inter-viewer and newsreader, with e-mails, telephone calls and other pathetically obscene communications. The stalker's story was that Miss Turnbull had invited these attentions, a defence which even Soapy was having little difficulty in tearing apart.

In view of the respect Hilda had shown for her New Year's resolution, I did my best to stick to mine. I held open doors, rose from my seat in the Underground; I even, in a moment of temporary aberration, lifted my hat to an elderly male Judge, who looked at me as though I had gone harmlessly insane. In due course, I turned up at the charity dinner of Urchins Anonymous, a glittering occasion in a City Livery Hall (the Ancient Order of Button-makers), and as we sipped champagne under the chandeliers, and I saw many cheerful pink faces over so many stretched white shirt fronts, and so many female necks – some, I have no doubt, rejuvenated by tactful surgery – decorated with rows of pearls, and as I looked up at the portraits of so many well-fed Masters of the Button-makers, I thought of the ten-year-old girl whose bedroom was the church steps, and the sleeping boy with a dog for a hot-water bottle. I supposed, after all, that the money raised by lobster salad and rack of lamb, Château Talbot and Rumpole's old jokes was of more use to children in flight from abusive stepfathers, missing mothers or even the police than no money at all.

It was over the champagne and canapés that I saw her, a woman not to be outdone by any of them in the matter of pearls on the neck, her black dress revealing an expanse of white back. The contrast was emphasized by a white lock in her otherwise raven hair. She came up to me, smiling, and was introduced by the Director of UA.

'Mr Rumpole, this is Marcia Endersley. One of our tireless voluntary workers. She organizes our urchin outings.'

'Oh, but I recognize Mr Rumpole.' The Endersley smile was charming, her voice low and vibrating with amusement. 'He offered me his seat, when I was bringing the urchins back from the Harry Potter film.'

'And you wouldn't take it,' I remembered.

'I thought your need was probably greater than mine. I hear you're going to give us some of your legal jokes. I'm sure they'll go down terribly well.'

She was smiling at me as she said it, but I had the distinct feeling that she was, in some obscure and subtle way, taking the piss.

Fashions in crime are as changeable as the length of skirts, popular music or the food in so-called smart restaurants. Every year or so, the government picks a favourite crime, which, so it is said, is likely to rot the foundations of society and cause universal anarchy. It regularly promises to 'crack

down' on the offence of the day, even to the extent of mandatory life sentences. When I was a young white-wig it was
frauds on the Post Office and the stealing of stamps, then it
was the trashing of telephone kiosks. Later, spraying graffiti
on the walls of multi-storey car parks and high-rise flats was
temporarily regarded as worse than manslaughter. At other
moments of recent history it has been mugging, stealing
mobile telephones and the theft of expensive cars.

At that time, after I had emerged from the dreaded Primrose Path Home, the crime of the day was nicking articles
from passengers on the Underground. The opportunities for
theft were numerous down the Tube, and ever more rarely
interrupted by the arrival of trains. In the crowds that packed
every platform it was easy to deprive the waiting customers of
their handbags, wallets and detachable jewellery. All this had
led to many stern warnings from the Home Secretary and
instructions to Judges to treat Underground theft as ranking
somewhere between matricide and High Treason in the hit
list of high crimes and misdemeanours.

'Theft of a wallet in an Underground station, Mr Rumpole,'
our clerk Henry said when he handed me the brief. I received
it with no high hopes of an easy victory or a lenient sentence.
'Thank you, Henry,' I said, 'for nothing very much at all. By
the way, you're not looking particularly happy this morning.'

'It's that Miss Gribble, Mr Rumpole.' Henry sat down des-
pondently in my clients' chair. 'Just who does she think she is?'

'I suppose she thinks she's Miss Gribble, otherwise known
as Luci with an "i". Who else could she possibly be?'

'Director of Marketing and Administration. She wants to
see my diary. She wants to be kept informed about fees on a
weekly basis. She says she wants me to self-assess.'

'She wants you to what?'

'Write an essay, like we did at school. About myself. My

strengths and my weaknesses. Quite frankly, Mr Rumpole, I haven't got the time for it. Do you think she's after my job?'

'I shouldn't think so. Anyway you can leave Luci with her "i" to me. She was a great help in a case I won without even going to Court.' I was referring, of course, to the Primrose Path affair. 'I'll have a word with her.' I looked at the brief, which bore the familiar title *R*. v. *Timson*, and, as I read through the statements, my confidence began to ebb away. I might be able to smooth the troubled waters that ran between our clerk and the new Marketing Director, but yet another larceny at a Tube station might prove more than I could manage.

My client in the case Henry had handed me was young Trevor Timson, a youth who had shown, by his previous convictions, little talent for the family business of ordinary, decent crime. His situation was not made more hopeful by my instructions from our solicitor, Bonny Bernard, who had come to the conclusion that the best we could do for the client was a plea in mitigation, if we could persuade him to put his hands up. And then, flipping through the papers, I saw something which gave us, if not hope, at least more than a glimmer of interest.

The facts of the case were alarmingly simple. It happened around six o'clock one weekday evening when the Tube station was crowded with released office workers. There had been numerous cases of dipped-into handbags, emptied hip pockets and pinched purses at that particular station, so the railway police were inconspicuously alert. Two of them were present in the lift when Mr Hornby, a company director who prided himself on his use of public transport, felt a fluttering disturbance in his breast pocket and found his wallet flown away. Being an old-fashioned sort of company director he called out 'Stop, thief!' and the railway policeman in the lift detained the passengers. Trevor Timson was unhesitantly denounced by a witness who said she saw him take the wallet, which was then found intact in his half-open shoulder bag. It contained three hundred pounds in crisp twenties.

So Bernard and I sat in the Brixton Prison interview room with the young sprig of the Timson family, who had been denied bail because of the number of his previous convictions.

'It's no good, Trevor,' Bonny Bernard said. 'We've got to chuck in our hand. The prosecution's got a cast-iron witness.'

To me, the phrase 'cast-iron witness' represented a challenge – particularly when the name on that witness statement was Marcia Endersley.

'This wonderful witness who says she saw you take the money,' I asked Trevor. 'Alone, was she? Or was someone with her?'

'Lots of kids.'

'What?'

'She had a party of kids with her. They were all excited and chattering. Like she was taking them out for a school treat.'

I sat in the interview room and I saw it again. The smiling woman, hanging on to a strap, and the boy looking up at her, offering her a present in gratitude for being taken out. A bar of chocolate, was it? Or sweets? It didn't look like sweets.

'So it's got to be a plea, Trevor.' Bernard was prepared to throw in the towel as cheerfully as possible, but I ventured to disagree.

'No, it's not. Never plead guilty. Let that be your New Year's resolution, Bonny Bernard.'

As we walked away across the prison yard, Bernard seemed pained at my brisk dismissal of his order to run up the white flag of surrender.

'I didn't want to argue the case, Mr Rumpole, not in front of the client. You say fight it. But what the devil do you imagine we're going to fight it with?'

'The wallet,' I said.

'The wallet? We can hardly call a wallet to give evidence.'

'Oh yes we can. Talk to your friends in the Crown Prosecution Service. See if it's been kept carefully, as an exhibit. Then persuade them to send it to forensic for a fingerprint test. We'll need to know about all the prints, and whether they come from known offenders.'

'Our client's a known offender.'

'So he is, Bonny Bernard, and that's why we must be particularly careful to see he doesn't get sent down for a crime he didn't do.'

'I still think we ought to plead guilty and throw ourselves on the mercy of the Court.'

'Would you say that,' I asked him, 'if we had to throw ourselves on the mercy of Judge Bullingham?'

And that seemed to shut the man up for the moment.

I would very much like you to undress for me completely. I long to pour custard over you, and after the custard, tomato ketchup. I imagine this and lots of other things and I hope you don't mind. I have no intention of forcing the custard on you. The whole incident would have to be entirely voluntary on your part. But if you feel as I do, I think we might have some really enjoyable times together.

The document on which this extraordinary message was written was, as I understand it, the 'print-out' of an e-mail Luci with an 'i' had received. She had shown it to me unasked and uninvited, explaining that, as we had become 'close' since the Primrose Path case, she valued my advice and wanted to know how she should take the message. 'Seeing who it comes from.'

When she told me, the news was like a sudden revelation that Her Majesty the Queen was joining a travelling circus.

'You don't really mean that Soapy Sam Ballard sent you this?'

'Chair sent it!'

'You're absolutely sure?'

'It was attached to an e-mail which said, "Perhaps you'd like to have a look at this and give me your reaction. S.B."'

'And have you given him your reaction?'

'That was what I wanted to ask your advice about. You've heard it all and done so many cases, and well, you've lived so long, Horace.'

'I never thought I'd live so long as to read Soapy Sam Ballard on the subject of custard.'

'Don't you like it, Horace?'

'Don't I like custard? In the right place, which is on a nice portion of baked jam roll, yes, I do. But not what is suggested here!'

'I think I told you, Horace,' Luci sounded almost shy, 'I do find our Chair hugely attractive.'

'I know. You told me that at your party, much to my amazement.'

'And of course he's married.'

'Then he ought to go home and pour custard over his wife.' I was, in this conversation, taking the moral high ground. 'I expect the ex-Old Bailey matron would send him away with a calming-down pill and a flea in his ear.' I speculated on the scene in vain. 'I can't really imagine it.'

Our tough Director of Marketing and Administration, who struck terror into the heart of Henry, seemed at a loss. 'The trouble is, I don't really know how to take this sort of approach. I mean, it's the sort of thing that might come up in the middle of a relationship. But I wouldn't have expected our Chair to have suggested it when – well, we've hardly got to know each other. Do you know what I mean?'

'I think I can guess.' I was surprised, well, I might even say gobsmacked, by the turn this conversation was taking. 'But surely this is something which should be discussed between the two of you. In some quiet place like, for instance, the corner table of Pommeroy's Wine Bar.'

'Horace, as I say, you've heard it all. Life, Love, Murder, Deception and –'

'Custard?'

'That too, probably. I just don't feel I can talk to our Chair about this at the moment. If I only knew how he really felt about me. Is it genuine, do you think? Or is it just –'

'Peculiar behaviour with the condiments?'

'I mean, you've known each other over the years. Has our Chair ever said anything to you?'

'About his feelings?'

'Yes.'

I looked at her – the black trouser suit, the glistening boots worn by the mistress of the flip chart, the ace targeter and measurer of achievement – and it seemed to me that Luci was in desperate need of help. 'Well, Soapy Sam hasn't taken me into his confidence about his feelings as yet. But I could always bring them up casually, in the course of conversation.'

'Oh, Horace, would you? Would you do that and let me know?'

'I might,' I said. 'But, on another subject, I don't think Henry's entirely happy about writing an essay on his strengths and weaknesses. I think he'd find it extremely embarrassing. He's used to assessing the strengths and weaknesses of barristers, but not to think about who he is.'

'He can forget that.' Luci was following my drift. 'If only you could have a word or two with our Chair.'

'I think I owe it to you,' I told her, 'for all the help you gave me in the Primrose Path affair. Meanwhile, what are you going to do about this e-mail he sent you?'

'I shall keep it,' she promised me. 'Whatever happens, I shall keep it as a souvenir.'

'Mr Rumpole, very good to see you back in your place in the Central Criminal Court. I trust you're fully recovered.'

'I was until I heard you welcoming me back,' I might have said, 'but now my breath has been entirely taken away by your Lordship's good wishes.' It was the second gob-smacking I had received in the course of a week. Soapy Sam's interest in unusual sex had been rapidly followed by an appearance before Judge Bullingham, but our raging Bull was now translated into a gentle, soft-eyed old cow who lowed at me with warm and welcoming words from the bench. Had I gone mad, or had the whole world been turned upside-down?

'I'm grateful to your Lordship,' I managed to say. 'I am, I suppose, as well as can be expected. Only, perhaps, a little surprised that your Lordship seems to have been missing me so much.'

'Always a pleasure to have you before me.' The old cow seemed to have taken to lying along with the personality change. 'And now perhaps we should get on with the trial of Mr Timson. Yes, Mr Prosser?'

So, after everyone had had a share of the New Bullingham warm welcome, Archie Prosser, the latest arrival at our Chambers, rose and opened his case. The story of the Underground station was told again in detail. Mr Hornby, the company director, entered the witness box and identified his stolen wallet, which was wrapped in cellophane and labelled 'Prosecution Exhibit A', being handled carefully as it had been examined for fingerprints. With some reluctance and a great deal of delay, the prosecution had agreed to providing the fingerprint evidence which had given me, when I read it, a good deal of quiet satisfaction. We had started after lunch and by four o'clock the New Bullingham beamed at us and said, 'Would it suit the convenience of you two gentlemen if we stop now and we hear the chief prosecution witness in the morning?' We beamed back and told him that would suit our convenience perfectly.

When I heard that the Bull was going to try the case at the Old Bailey, I thought it was because they wanted someone to crack down, in the most ruthless manner, on the fashionable crime of Underground wallet-pinching and that we were in for a blood-stained *corrida*. Having seen the New Bullingham, I ventured to ask his clerk, whom I saw, by chance, halfway through a pint of Guinness in Pommeroy's, whether the Old Judge was not in fact sickening for something?

'My Judge is not sickening for anything,' Bullingham's clerk was an imperturbable Scot, 'except the Lord Chancellor.'

'What's the Lord Chancellor got to do with it?'

'There've been complaints to the Lord Chancellor about my Judge's rudeness to witnesses and members of the Bar.'

'He was quite even-handed in his rudeness,' I agreed.

'My Judge,' the clerk was clearly loyal, 'was quite fair in that way. But the Lord Chancellor told him he wanted to hear no more of such complaints. Or else.'

'Or else what?'

'According to my Judge, the Lord Chancellor simply said "or else". So my Judge made a New Year's resolution.'

'To be polite to everybody?' I suggested.

'To be, Mr Rumpole,' the Scottish clerk drained his glass, 'absolutely charming to everyone, including yourself.'

'Hello, Rumpole. How can I help you?'

'I was thinking more in terms of helping you, Chair.'

'Our Marketing and Administration Director calls me that.'

'She calls you more than that, Ballard,' I assured him. 'And she really longs to call you "darling".'

'Rumpole!' Soapy Sam looked shocked. 'I have absolutely no idea what you're talking about.'

'I'm talking about the fact that Luci with an "i" finds you devastatingly attractive, and also the fact that there's no accounting for tastes.'

After meeting the old Bull's clerk in Pommeroy's, I had called into Chambers to give some thought to the next day's cross-examination in *R.* v. *Timson*. I noticed that Ballard's light was on. Having a delicate task to perform on behalf of the love-lorn Luci, I told myself that there was no time like the present and pushed open his door. I discovered him seated in front of his computer, manipulating his mouse and looking, as people engaged in this process always seem to do, with puzzled irritation at his screen. I settled myself in his clients' chair and the proceedings opened as set out above.

'What do you mean, Rumpole?'

'I mean that Luci with an "i" loves you, Ballard. She was extremely chuffed to get your e-mail. In fact, it's no exaggeration to say that she was over the moon about it.'

'I sent her an e-mail about contract cleaners for Chambers. She's considering sourcing a new firm for the task.'

I noticed that Ballard had learned to speak in Luci's language. This might be of some encouragement to her.

'It doesn't matter what she was "sourcing". She was excited by the attachment.'

'The attachment was a new firm's estimate.'

'Oh, come on, Ballard!' I might, as an old-fashioned legal hack, have added 'Don't fence with me!' 'You know your message didn't say that at all.'

'Of course it did. Anyway, how would you know, Rumpole?'

'Because she showed it to me.'

'She showed you the cleaners' estimate?'

'Nothing about the cleaners.'

'Well, what do you say it was then?'

'It was mainly about custard.'

'*Custard?*' The man seemed, for a moment, totally mystified. 'Why on earth should I be e-mailing our Marketing and Administration Director on the subject of custard?'

'Suppose you tell me.'

'I have absolutely no idea.'

'Could it be because you want to pour the stuff over her naked body?'

At which our Head of Chambers gave an earth-shaking groan, sank his face into his hands, called several times on his God and began, with every sign of panic, to activate his mouse in an agitated fashion while exclaiming, 'What an idiot I am! That's what I did! That's exactly what I did! What an idiot!'

I didn't quarrel with the description, but had to ask the question, 'What did you do, exactly?'

'It was a note for my case. Part of the letter the stalker was going to send to Jenny. I was preparing my cross-examination. I must have pressed the wrong button! What an idiot!'

'You mean you were going to cross-examine your stalker about the new office cleaners? That might have taken him by surprise.'

'Worse than that. I've made that terrible suggestion to Luci Gribble.'

'Don't worry.' Rumpole the conciliator moved in to settle the case. 'I don't think she found it so terrible. Curious. Perhaps unusual. She felt that it showed, at least, that you cared.'

'Cared?'

'I mean, that you were interested.'

'Of course I'm interested in Luci Gribble. She's a first-class business woman.'

'I think she wants you to see her as rather more than that.'

'I'll ring her immediately and tell her I made a horrible mistake.'

'Take my advice, Ballard. Don't do that. Whatever you do, don't tell her that it was all a horrible mistake.'

'Good heavens, Rumpole, why ever not?'

'Because she loves you, Ballard. She has tender feelings for you. She believes now that you have tender feelings for her.'

'Does pouring custard show tender feelings?'

'In certain circumstances it may. Yes. So what effect is it going to have on her if you tell her that your amorous message was just a horrible mistake?'

'What effect are you suggesting, Rumpole?'

'Devastation. Bitterness. Gloom. She'll forget her flip charts and muddle up her target figures and Administration and Marketing will fall into complete chaos.'

'So what shall I do?'

I was, I have to confess, touched. Ballard the Head of Chambers had become Ballard the client, anxious, indeed terrified, begging his brief to find a solution to an impossible case.

'Tell her you love her. And you couldn't resist telling her what you'd like to do with or without custard. But tell her that you're married to Matey and any hint of scandal would seriously damage the Chambers image. So you'll both just have to be extraordinarily brave about it. That way you won't come out as an idiot who can't manage his e-mail and she'll still feel loved.'

'Rumpole,' Soapy Sam still seemed sunk in gloom, 'I can't possibly tell her that.'

'Can't you? Why ever not?'

'Because it's not true.'

'Perhaps not, but at least it's kind.'

'All the same, I can't see myself saying it. I'd get it all wrong. It wouldn't be convincing.'

'What you need,' I had to tell him, 'is a decent barrister to represent you.'

'Oh, Rumpole.' The Head of Chambers' face lit up with gratitude. 'Would you really take it on?'

The next morning the bullring was, once again, bathed in sunshine. The Judge beamed on all of us, but kept his warmest smiles for Marcia Endersley in the witness box. She stood there, her white lock adding, it seemed, a sort of elegance and distinction to the proceedings, and described her voluntary work for Urchins Anonymous and her practice of taking groups of deprived, perhaps homeless children to museums and cinemas, 'to get them out of themselves and so they could forget their troubles'.

'And you did all this wonderful work,' the Bull marvelled, 'for no sort of financial reward?'

'My reward was seeing the children look happy, and interested, of course. It was a significant reward to see how a boy from a depressed and violent home could respond to the Elgin Marbles, my Lord.'

'Then may I say, Madam, this country needs a great many more women of your stamp. Too many people nowadays,' and here he looked, still smiling, at the assembled lawyers, 'think about nothing but their fees, and matters of that sort.'

The wonderful Marcia Endersley went through the sad story of the scene in the lift. Yes, she recognized the young man in the dock. She had seen him standing very close to Mr Hornby and, after a quick movement, stow a wallet away in his backpack. No, she had no doubts about all this. The besotted Bull hung on her every word, made copious notes of all she said and, when she had finished in chief, congratulated her warmly.

'We're all grateful to you, Madam, for the clear way you have given your evidence. If only we had more witnesses like you. Now I expect Mr Rumpole has a few questions for you. I'm sure he won't detain you for long. And then you can get back to the wonderful work you're doing for those unfortunate children.'

'Oh, I know Mr Rumpole.' Marcia was smiling at me. 'We met at a UA dinner. Mr Rumpole told some jokes.'

'Then he's indeed a fortunate man to have met you and I hope, on this occasion, he'll spare us the jokes. Yes, Mr Rumpole.'

'What sort of entertainments did you take the children to?' I asked my first question with a certain amount of cold detachment, determined to break up the love-in between the Judge and the witness.

'They enjoyed the Science Museum. And the London Eye, of course. I'd take parties to the cinema, if the film was suitable.'

'And what sort of films did you consider suitable? Thrillers? Crime stories?'

'I wouldn't take them to see films about crime.'

'I'm sure you took them to excellent films,' the old Bull cooed. '*The Sound of Music* – I remember that was a particularly charming one.'

'Of course,' Marcia Endersley rewarded the Judge with a sympathetic smile, 'there aren't too many films like that about nowadays.'

'Pity you didn't take them to something more exciting,' I suggested. 'Children like a bit of crime, don't they?'

'Mr Rumpole!' There was a distinct trace of the old roaring Bull in the way the Judge now uttered my name. Was the New Year's resolution being put under some strain? 'It may be your time is spent dealing with the more sordid side of life . . . but this good lady' (another beaming smile at her) 'was trying to show the children a better world.'

'Oh, I don't think you should knock crime, my Lord. After all, we both make our living out of it.'

There was a little stir of laughter from the Jury, which caused the Bull to lower his head and charge. The New Year was clearly a thing of the past, and his promises to the Lord Chancellor forgotten.

'That was an outrageous remark, Mr Rumpole!' he exploded. 'Quite outrageous!'

'I'm sorry. I was under the impression we were both being paid to take part in a criminal trial. With your Lordship's permission, I'd like to continue my cross-examination.' And without further apology, I turned to the witness. 'Mrs Endersley, did you take different children out on each occasion, or was it the same group?'

'It changed, of course. But there were some children I got to know really well.'

'I'm sure there were. And, on the whole, did you find them easy to control? I mean, they did what you told them?'

'I'm sure they found it very easy to obey *you*, Madam.' The Judge looked as though he'd be delighted to do exactly what Marcia Endersley told him.

'If we could come to the facts of this case.' I was determined to put an end to this cross-Court flirtation. 'When you say you saw my client take the wallet, were you wearing gloves?'

'Mr Rumpole! What on earth's the relevance of that question? Are you deliberately trying to waste the Court's time?' The Bull charged in again, all resolutions cast aside.

'If your Lordship would allow the witness to answer, you might discover.'

'Yes, of course I wore gloves.' Marcia Endersley looked down on us from the height of the witness box and seemed determined to put an end to our bickering. 'I always wear gloves on the Tube. It's so terribly dirty.'

'Of course it is,' the Bull hurried to agree. 'Look at the witness, Mr Rumpole. Is she not perfectly turned out? Does not her appearance speak of her fastidious nature? Why should she not wear gloves?'

'Oh, I've no doubt they were very useful, weren't they?' I did my best to ignore the Bull and speak to the witness as though there were no Judge to support her. 'For your particular journeys on the Underground. I take it that Trevor Timson, the young man in the dock, was not wearing gloves on this occasion?'

'I hardly think so. I expect the only sort of gloves your client wears are boxing gloves, Mr Rumpole.'

Members of the Jury laughed obediently at the Judge's apology for a joke. I could afford to be patient. I was holding the fingerprint report which I told the Judge had been agreed by Archie Prosser for the prosecution.

'I can't see what fingerprints have got to do with this case,' the Bull rumbled, and I told him that if he listened very carefully he might find out. It was a relief, I somehow felt, to be back to the old days of the *corrida*, when the Bull had to be handled with courage by an experienced matador. Dealing with a charming Bull had been an unsettling and alarming experience.

'Would it interest you to know that there are none of Trevor Timson's fingerprints on the wallet,' I asked Marcia. 'And yet you say you saw him take it from Mr Hornby's jacket?'

'It was very quick. A matter of seconds.'

'I'm sure it was. And it must have been done by magic. He must have spirited the thing through the air without touching it.'

Now the Jury had stopped laughing and were looking at the witness with renewed interest.

'I don't know how he got it out.' She did her best to look bored with my questions.

'Let me tell you a little more about the fingerprints. The owner of the wallet had left his, of course. But there were some other prints, rather small, left by someone with a police record. A young boy, no more than twelve years old, who had a conviction for stealing. Was he one of your Anonymous Urchins? A boy called Chris Hemmings. Did you take him out on one of these trips?'

'I've no idea. I can't remember all their names.'

'Can't you really? But you remembered to wear gloves. Was that so you would leave no fingerprints on stolen wallets?'

'Mr Rumpole!' The horns were lowered and the Bull was pawing the ground. 'In all my years on the Bench I have never heard such an outrageous suggestion. I think you should consider your own position very carefully unless you withdraw it. Are you seriously suggesting that this lady, of unblemished character, who devotes her spare time to taking out deprived inner-city children to such places as the Science Museum, actually stole this man's wallet? On the Underground?'

'She didn't steal it, my Lord. One of the children she carefully trained, and no doubt rather inadequately paid, stole it. She received it, though. And when she saw that the railway police were going to make a search she got rid of it, in the nearest open bag she saw, which happened to be Trevor Timson's. And then she denounced him as a thief.' I thought I'd said quite enough to the Judge and turned to that selfless philanthropist, the Mrs Fagin of the Underground. 'Is that the truth?'

'That is absolute nonsense!'

She was looking only a little less composed, but her hand grabbed the rail of the witness box as though she had a sudden fear of falling. I paused as I remembered what I had seen when I offered her my seat. A young boy who was giving her something. Not sweets. Not a message. I remembered the colour. Was it – I felt sure now that it was – the faded brown of folding money. Before the Bull could roar again, I spoke to the witness.

'Let's examine it, shall we? And see whether it's nonsense or not. You took these children out to museums and occasional cinemas. Perhaps gave them tea. Who paid?'

'I've told you. I paid.'

'So they had no occasion to give you money.'

'None at all.'

'You're saying they didn't have money with them?'

'None at all.'

'So if anyone was to say they'd seen a boy hand you what looked like a wad of tenners, that would be untrue?'

'That would be quite untrue. Yes.'

'That would be quite untrue.' The Bull was making a careful note of the answer and I had a bad moment, thinking I would have to go into the witness box and tell the Jury what I had seen: a small, gap-toothed, grinning boy handing her bank notes, which she grasped quickly in a gloved hand.

It never came to that. Halfway through that morning, Archie Prosser, for the prosecution, asked for an adjournment. A couple of children had been caught in an attempted handbag-pinching on the Circle Line. They had told the whole story of Mrs Endersley's tireless work for inner-city youth and a surprise visit to her flat in Primrose Hill revealed a large quantity of handbags, wallets, watches, and money. The trial of the confident woman, who kept her white lock because she was so sure she'd never have to be identified, is fixed for next month. I doubt very much whether she'll want me to defend her.

What I find hard to forget is the sight of the boy asleep in a doorway with a dog. Was he, perhaps, one of Marcia Endersley's failed pickpockets, sent back by her to the anonymity of the streets so that he couldn't be questioned? I think of the grand dinner in the Ancient Order of Button-makers and the girl sleeping every night on the church steps, and wonder if the children of Ignorance and Want must always be with us. Or, worse still, always be used.

Briefed by Soapy Sam Ballard, I told Luci of his deep love for her and his resolve to abstain, for the sake of the image of Chambers, from thoughts of a deeper intimacy or anything connected with custard. She took the news bravely and could be caught staring at the Chair, during Chambers meetings, with love and understanding.

And, one morning, Hilda and I returned to a subject which seemed to have dominated recent events.

'I really don't know whether it's worth making New Year's resolutions,' I told her at breakfast. 'You know why Trevor Timson was on the Underground when he got arrested?'

'No. Why?'

'He'd made a New Year's resolution to visit his Probation Officer, a duty he occasionally skipped. On the other hand –'

'What's the other hand?'

'If you hadn't kept me to a New Year's resolution to offer my seat to ladies on trains, I'd never have seen those stolen tenners popped into Mrs Endersley's welcoming gloves.'

'And what about *my* New Year's resolution?' Hilda looked

doubtful. 'Now I come to think about it, I'm not sure it was necessary. Dodo Mackintosh sometimes talks an awful lot of nonsense.'

'I quite agree.'

'I'm not really bossy, am I?'

'Perish the thought.'

'Good. I'm glad you said that. And by the way, you've got to stop eating all that fried food at breakfast. You're putting on far too much weight.'

So we were in another year when my fry-up, once again, would be taken at the Tastee Bite in Fleet Street. All new resolutions would fade into the past and normal life, for better or for worse, would be resumed.

Rumpole and the Scales of Justice

'The Scales of Justice have tipped in the wrong direction. That's all I'm saying, Jenny. Now it's all in favour of the defence, and that makes our job so terribly hard. I mean, we catch the villains and, ten to one, they walk away from Court laughing.'

Bob Durden, resplendent in his Commander's uniform, appeared in the living-room of Froxbury Mansions in the Gloucester Road. He was in conversation with Jenny Turnbull, the hard-hitting and astute interviewer on the *Up to the Minute* programme.

'You've got to admit he's right, Rumpole.' She Who Must Be Obeyed could be as hard-hitting and astute as Jenny. 'Things have gone too far. It's all in favour of the defence.'

'Why don't you – and the Commander, of course – try defending some unfortunate innocent before the Mad Bull down the Old Bailey? You'd have a Judge who's longing to pot your client, and is prepared to use every trick in the book to get the Jury on his side, and a prosecutor who can afford to make all the enquiries and is probably keeping quiet about evidence that's slightly favourable to the defence, and a Jury out for revenge because someone stole their car radios. Then you'd find out how much things are slanted in favour of the defence.'

'Oh, do be quiet.' She Who Must didn't have time for a legal argument. 'I'm trying to listen to the Commander.'

Bob Durden ruled the forces of law and order in an area, half crowded countryside, half sprawling suburbs, to the north of London. When the old East End died, and its streets and squares became inhabited by upwardly mobile media persons, ethnic restaurants and the studios of conceptual artists, it was to Commander Durden's patch that the forces of lawlessness moved. He was a large, broad-shouldered, loose-lipped man who spoke as though he were enjoying some secret joke.

'But aren't there cases when the police haven't been exactly on the side of the law?' said Jenny Turnbull.

Well done, Jenny, I thought. It's about time someone asked that question.

Hilda, however, took a different view. 'That girl,' she said, 'should learn to show respect to the people she's interviewing. After all, the man is a Commander. She could at least be polite.'

'She's far too polite, in my opinion. If I were cross-examining I'd be a good deal less respectful.' I addressed the television set directly. 'When are your officers going to stop bribing witnesses by putting them up in luxurious, all-expenses-paid hotels, and improving on confession statements?'

'Do be quiet, Rumpole! You're worse than that Turnbull woman, interrupting that poor man.'

'You know who I blame, Jenny? I blame the lawyers. The "learned friends" in wigs. Are they part of the Justice System? Part of the Injustice System, if you want my honest opinion.' The Commander spoke from the television set, in a tone of amused contempt to which I took the greatest exception. 'It's all a game to them, isn't it? Get your guilty client off and collect a nice fat-cat fee from Legal Aid for your trouble.'

'Have you got any particular barrister in mind?' Jenny Turnbull clearly scented a story.

'Well, Jenny, I'm not naming names. But there are regular

defenders down at the Old Bailey and they'll know who I mean. There was a case some time ago. Theft in the Underground. The villain, with a string of previous convictions, had the stolen wallet in his backpack. Bang to rights, you might say. This old brief pulled a few defence tricks and the culprit walked free. We get to know them, "Counsel for the Devious Defence", and quite frankly there's very little we can do about them.'

'Absolute rubbish!' I shouted fruitlessly at the flickering image of the Commander. 'Trevor Timson got off because he was entirely innocent. Are you saying that everyone with previous convictions should be found guilty regardless of the facts? Is *that* what you're saying?'

'It's no good at all you shouting at him, Rumpole.' Hilda was painfully patient. 'He can't hear a word you're saying.' As usual, She Who Must Be Obeyed was maddeningly correct.

A considerable amount of time passed, a great quantity of Château Thames Embankment flowed down parched legal throats in Pommeroy's Wine Bar, a large number of custodial sentences were handed out to customers down the Bailey, and relatively few of those detained there went off laughing. Gradually, as the small shoots of promise appear when spring follows winter, my practice began to show signs of an eventual bloom. I progressed from petty thievery (in the case of the New Year's Resolutions) to more complicated fraud, from actual to grievous bodily harm, and from an affray outside a bingo hall to a hard-fought manslaughter in a sauna. It was in the months before I managed to play my part in the richly rewarding case – in satisfaction rather than money – that I am about to record. I was sitting in my Chambers room enjoying an illicit small cigar (Soapy Sam Ballard was still in the business of banning minor pleasures) and leafing through *The*

Oxford Book of English Verse in search of a suitable quotation to use in my final speech in a case of alleged gross indecency in Snaresbrook, when a brisk knock at the door was followed by the entrance of none other that Dame Phillida Erskine-Brown, once the much-admired Portia of our Chambers, now the appealing occupant of Judicial Benches from the Strand and Ludgate Circus to Manchester and Exeter Crown Court.

'You'll never guess what I've seen, Rumpole! Never in a million years!' Her Ladyship was in what can only be described as a state of outrage, and whatever she had seen had clearly not been a pretty sight. 'I just dropped in to tell Claude he'll have to look after the children tonight because I've got a dinner with the Lord Chancellor and the babysitter's got evening classes.'

'All part of the wear and tear of married life?'

'It's not that. It's what I saw in the clerk's room. In front of Henry and Denise. Claude, flagrantly in the arms of another woman!'

'When you say in the arms of –' I merely asked for clarification. 'What were they doing, exactly? I take it they weren't kissing each other?'

'Not that. No. They were hugging.'

'Well, that's all right then.' I breathed a sigh of relief. 'If they were only hugging.'

'What do you mean, "That's all right then"? I said "Am I disturbing something?" and walked straight out of the clerk's room and came to see you, Rumpole. I must say I expected you to take this extraordinary conduct of Claude's rather more seriously.'

I couldn't help remembering the time when Dame Phillida, once the nervous pupil whom I'd found in my room in tears, now a Judge of the Queen's Bench, had herself tugged a little at the strict bonds of matrimony and conceived an inexplicable passion for a Doctor Tom Gurnley, a savagely punitive right-wing Tory MP who believed in mandatory prison sentences for the first whiff of cannabis, and whom I had had to defend in the case of the Camberwell Carrot. I suppose it wasn't an exact parallel – the Learned Judge had not been discovered embracing the old hanger and flogger in our clerk's room.

Now that the Erskine-Browns' marriage seemed to have sailed into calmer waters, I was unwilling to rock the boat. I offered an acceptable solution.

'Exactly whom was your husband hugging?'

'I couldn't see much of her. She seemed to have blonde hair. Not entirely convincing, I thought.'

'A black trouser suit? Shiny boots?'

'I think so, now you mention it.'

'Then that would be our new Director of Marketing and Administration.'

'I believe Claude told me you have one of them. So that makes it perfectly all right, does it?' I could see that the Judge was not entirely satisfied. 'Is part of her job description snogging my husband?'

'Not snogging. Hugging.'

'All right then, hugging. Is that her job – is that what you're saying?'

'Provided it's Thursday.'

'Rumpole! Are you feeling quite well?'

'Her name is Luci. She spells it with an "i".'

'Does she do that to irritate people?'

'That might well be part of it. And she had the idea that we should all hug each other at work on Thursday. She said it would improve our corporate spirit and lead to greater harmony in the workplace.'

'You mean you *all* hug each other?'

'If you look on the noticeboard, you'll see that Soapy Sam Ballard has commended the idea to 'Everyone at Number 4 Equity Court'. He's very pro-Luci because I told him she fancied him.'

'Rumpole! Has the whole world gone mad?'

'Only on Thursdays. That's when we're meant to hug each other. On Fridays Luci has decided that we dress down.'

'What does that mean, exactly?'

'It means that Ballard comes in wearing jeans and a red sweater with black diamonds on it. Oh, and white gym shoes, of course.'

'You mean trainers?'

'Probably.'

'Do you dress down, Rumpole?'

'Certainly not. I can't afford the wardrobe. I stick to my working clothes: black jacket and striped trousers.'

'I thought I saw Claude sneak out of the house in jeans. He hasn't told me.'

'Your Claude has a nervous disposition. I expect he was afraid you'd laugh at him.'

'I certainly would. And about the hugging. Do you hug, Rumpole?'

'Embrace our clerk Henry? Snuggle up to Ballard? Certainly not! I told them hugging always brought me out in a rash. I have a special dispensation not to do it for health reasons. It's like taking the vegetarian dish.'

'What did Ballard say when you told him you wouldn't hug?'

'He said I could just say "Good Morning" in an extra cheerful manner. Have I set your mind at rest?'

'I suppose so.' Phillida seemed reluctant to abandon a genuine cause for complaint against the unfortunate Claude. 'Provided he doesn't embrace that woman too enthusiastically. She's far too old for that haircut.'

'It was pure coincidence you came in at that moment,' I told her. 'If you'd come in ten minutes later you'd have found him wrapped around Hoskins, a balding, middle-aged man with numerous daughters.'

'You're always counsel for the defence, aren't you, Rumpole?'

'I can only say that, in any situation which looks guilty, I can sometimes offer an innocent alternative to the Jury.'

'Bob Durden would call that another trick of the defender's trade. Did you see him on the television the other night?'

'I certainly did. And I just wish I had the chance to wake the Commander up to the reality of life when you're on trial at the Old Bailey.'

At this the learned and beautiful Judge looked at me with some amusement, but my chance came sooner than either of us expected.

The earth-shaking news was read out by Hilda from her tabloid newspaper one morning in Froxbury Mansions. She looked seriously upset.

'Feet of clay, Rumpole! That sensible policeman we saw on *Up to the Minute* turns out to have feet of clay!'

I had been trying to catch up with some last-minute instructions in a fairly complicated long firm fraud when She Who Must handed me the paper, from which the face of Bob Durden loomed solemn and severe beneath his cap. The headline, however, suggested that not only were his feet clay but the rest of him was by no means perfect senior-police-officer material. The Commander had been arrested on no less a charge than taking part in a conspiracy to murder. It took a good half-minute before I was able to suppress an unworthy tendency to gloat.

Of course I read every detail of the extraordinary case, in

which it was suggested that the scourge of defence lawyers had been prepared to pay a contract killer to do away with a local doctor; but I was sure that the last member of the Bar he would call upon to defend him was that devious Rumpole who spent his life helping guilty villains walk free from court-rooms laughing triumphantly at the police. So the Commander took his place at the back of my mind, but I was on the lookout for developments in the newspapers.

One memorable day, Ballard appeared in my room with a look of sublime satisfaction and the air of a born commander about to issue battle orders. I have to say that he had smartened up a good deal since I let him know that our Director of Marketing and Administration nursed tender feelings for him. He had invested in a new suit, his hair was more dashingly trimmed by a Unisex Stylist, and he arrived in a chemical haze of after-shave which happily evaporated during the course of the day.

'This, Rumpole,' he told me, 'will probably be the most famous case of my career. The story, you'll have to admit, is quite sensational.'

'What's happened, Ballard?' I had no wish to fuel Soapy Sam's glowing self-satisfaction. 'What've you landed now? Another seven days before the rating tribunal?'

'I have been offered, Rumpole,' the man was blissfully unaware of any note of sarcasm; he was genuinely proud of his eventful days in Court with rateable values, 'the leading brief for the defence in *R. v. Durden*. It is, of course, tragic that a fine police officer should fall so low.'

Of course, I realized that the case called for a QC (Queer Customer is what I call them) and, as I have said, that the defendant policeman would never turn to Rumpole in a time of trouble. I couldn't help, however, feeling a momentary stab of jealousy at the thought of Ballard landing such a front-page, sensational cause célèbre.

'He hasn't fallen low yet.' I thought it right to remind our Head of Chambers of the elementary rules of our trade. 'And he won't until the Jury come back to Court and pronounce him guilty. It's your job to make sure they never do that.'

'I know, Rumpole.' Soapy Sam looked enormously brave. 'I realize I have taken on an almost superhuman task and a tremendous responsibility. But I've been able to do you a good turn.'

'What sort of good turn, exactly?' I was doubtful about Ballard's gifts, but then he told me.

'You see, the Commander went to a local solicitor, Henry Crozier – we were at university together – and Henry knew that Durden wouldn't want any flashy sort of clever-dick, defence QC. The sort he's spoken out against so effectively on the television.'

'You mean he picked you because you're not a clever dick?'

'Dependable, Rumpole. And, I flatter myself, trusted by the Courts. And as I believe your practice has slowed down a bit since . . .'

'You mean since I died?'

'Since you came back to us, I persuaded Henry Crozier to give you the Junior brief. Naturally, in a case of this importance, I shall do most of it myself. If the chance arises you might be able to call some formal, undisputed evidence. And of course you'll take a note of my cross-examination. You'll be capable of that, won't you?'

'My near-death experience has left me more than capable of conducting the most difficult trial.'

'Don't worry, old fellow.' Soapy Sam was smiling at me in a way I found quite unendurable. 'You won't be called on to do anything like that.'

*

As I have said, Commander Durden's patch was an area not far from London, and certain important villains had moved into it when London's East End was no longer the crime capital. They ran chains of minicab firms, clubs and wine bars, they were shadowy figures behind Thai restaurants and garden centres. They dealt in hard drugs and protection rackets in what may have seemed, to a casual observer, to be the heart of Middle England. And no one could have been more Middle English than Doctor Petrus Wakefield, who carried on his practice in Chivering. This had once been a small market town with a broad main street, and had now had its heart ripped out to make way for a pedestrian precinct with a multi-storey car park, identical shops and strict regulations against public meetings or yobbish behaviour.

Doctor Wakefield, I was to discover, was a pillar of this community, tall, good-looking, in his fifties. He was a leading light in the Amateur Dramatic Society, chairman of various charities and the doting husband of Judy, pretty, blonde and twenty years his junior. Their two children, Simon and Sarah, were high achievers at a local private school. Nothing could have been more quietly successful, some might even say boring, than the Wakefields' lives up to the moment when, so it was alleged, Commander Bob Durden took out a contract on the doctor's life.

The local police force, as local forces did, relied on a body of informers, many of whom came with long strings of previous convictions attached to them, to keep them abreast of the crimes and misdemeanours which took place in this apparently prosperous and law-abiding community. According to my instructions, the use of police informers hadn't been entirely satisfactory. There was a suspicion that some officers had been using them to form relationships with local villains, to warn them of likely searches and arrests and to arrange, in the worst cases, for a share of the spoils.

Commander Bob Durden was commended in the local paper 'for the firm line he was taking and the investigation he was carrying out into the rumours of police corruption'. One of the informers involved was a certain Len 'the Silencer' Luxford, so called because of his old connections with quietened firearms, but who had, it seemed, retired from serious crime and started a window-cleaning business in Chivering. He was still able occasionally to pass on information, heard in pubs and clubs from his old associates, to the police.

According to Detective Inspector Mynot, Bob Durden met Len the Silencer in connection with his enquiry into police informers. Unusually, he saw Len alone and without any other officer being present. According to Len's statement, the Commander then offered him five thousand pounds to 'silence' Doctor Wakefield, half down and half on completion of the task, the choice of weapons being left to the Silencer. Instead of carrying out these fatal instructions, Len, who owed, he said, a debt of gratitude to the doctor for the way he'd treated Len's mother, warned his prospective victim, who reported the whole matter to Detective Inspector Mynot. The case might have been thought slender if Doctor Wakefield hadn't been able to produce a letter from the Commander he'd found in his wife's possession, telling Judy how blissfully happy they might be together if Petrus Wakefield vanished from the face of the earth.

Such were the facts which led to Bob Durden, who thought all Old Bailey defence hacks nothing but spanners in the smooth works of justice, employing me, as Ballard had made painfully clear, as his *junior* counsel.

★

'I'm afraid I have to ask you this. Did you write this letter to Doctor Wakefield's wife?'

'I wrote the letter, yes. She must have left it lying about somewhere.'

'You said you'd both be happy if Doctor Wakefield vanished from the face of the earth. Why did you want that?'

We were assembled in Ballard's room for a conference. The Commander, on bail and suspended from his duties on full pay, wearing a business suit, was looking smaller than in his full-dress appearance on the television screen. His solicitor, Mr Crozier, a local man and apparently Ballard's old university friend, had a vaguely religious appearance to go with his name; that is to say he had a warm smile, a crumpled grey suit and an expression of sadness at the sins of the world. His client's answer to my leader's question did absolutely nothing to cheer him up.

'You see, Mr Ballard, we were in love. You write silly things when you're in love, don't you?' The bark of authority we had heard on television was gone. The Commander's frown had been smoothed away. He spoke quietly, almost gently.

'And send silly e-mails to people who fancy you,' I hoped Soapy Sam might say, but of course he didn't. Instead he said, in his best Lawyers as Christians tone of deep solemnity, 'You, a married man, wrote like that to a married woman?'

'I'm afraid things like that do happen, Mr Ballard. Judy Wakefield's an extremely attractive woman.'

There had been a picture of her in the paper, a small, smiling mother of two who had, apparently, fallen in love with a policeman.

'And you, a police commander, wrote in that way to a doctor's wife?'

'I'm not particularly proud of how we behaved. But as I

told you, we were crazy about each other. We just wanted to be together, that was all.'

Ballard apparently remained deeply shocked, so I ventured to ask a question.

'When you wrote that you'd both be much happier if he vanished from the face of the earth, you weren't suggesting the doctor would die. You simply meant that he'd get out of her life and leave you to each other. Wasn't that it?'

'Yes, of course.' The Commander looked grateful. 'You're putting it absolutely correctly.'

'That's all right. It's just a defence barrister's way of putting it,' I was glad to be able to say.

Soapy Sam, however, still looked displeased. 'You can be assured,' he told our client, 'that I shall be asking you the questions, Mr Durden. Mr Rumpole will be with me to take note of the evidence. I'm quite sure the Jury won't want to hear sordid details of your matrimonial infidelity. It won't do our case any good at all if we dwell on that aspect of the matter.'

Ballard was turning over his papers, preparing to venture on to another subject.

'If you don't mind my saying so,' I interrupted, I hoped not too rudely, 'I think the Commander's affair with the doctor's wife the most important factor in the case, whichever way you look at it. I think we need to know all we can about it.'

At this Ballard gave a thin, watery smile and once again bleated, 'As I said I shall be asking the questions in Court. Now, we can obviously attack the witness Luxford on the basis of his previous convictions, which include two charges of dishonesty. If you could just take us through your meeting with this man . . .'

'Did you use him much as an informer?' I interrupted, much to Ballard's annoyance.

But the Commander answered me, 'Hardly at all. In fact, I think it was a year or two since he'd given us anything. I thought he'd more or less retired. That was why I was surprised when he came to me with all that information about one of my officers.'

Durden then went through his conversation with the Silencer, which contained no reference to any proposed assassination. This was made quite clear in our instructions, so I excused myself and slipped out of the door, counted up to two hundred in my head and re-entered to tell Soapy Sam that our Director of Marketing and Administration wished to see him without delay on a matter of extreme urgency. Our leader excused himself, straightened his tie, patted down his hair and made for the door.

'Now then,' I gave our instructing solicitor some quick instructions as I settled myself in Ballard's chair, 'have a look at our client's bank statements, Mr Crozier. Make sure that an inexplicable two and a half thousand didn't get drawn out in cash. If the account's clean tell the prosecution you'll disclose it providing they give us the good Doctor's.'

'Very well, Mr Rumpole, but why . . . ?'

'Never mind about why for the moment. You might help me a bit more about Doctor Wakefield. I suppose he is pretty well known in the town. Has he practised there for years?'

'A good many years. I think he started off in London. A practice in the East End – Bethnal Green, that's what he told us. Apparently a pretty rough area. Then he came out to Chivering.'

'To get away from the East End?'

'I don't know. He always said he enjoyed working there.'

'I'm sure he did. One other thing. He is a pillar of the Dramatic Society, isn't he? What sort of parts does he play?'

'Oh, leads.' The solicitor seemed to brighten up considerably when he told me about it. 'The Chivering Mummers are rather ambitious, you know. We did a quite creditable *Othello* when it was the A-level play.'

'And the Doctor took the lead? You're not suggesting he blacked up? That's not allowed nowadays.'

'Oh, no. The *other* great part.'

'Of course.' I made a mental note. 'That's most interesting.'

A minute later, a flustered Ballard returned to the room and I moved politely out of his chair. He hadn't been able to find Luci with an 'i' anywhere in Chambers, a fact which came as no surprise to me at all.

When I got home to Froxbury Mansions, I happened to mention, over the shepherd's pie and cabbage, that Commander Bob Durden had admitted to an affair with the Doctor's attractive and much younger wife.

'That comes as no surprise to me at all,' Hilda told me. 'As soon as he appeared on the television I was sure there was something fishy about that man.'

I was glad to discover that, when it comes to telling lies, Hilda can do it as brazenly as any of my clients.

In the weeks before the trial, I thought a good deal about Doctor Petrus Wakefield. Petrus was, you will have to admit, a most unusual Christian name, perhaps bestowed by a pedantic Latin master and his classically educated wife on a child they didn't want to call anything as commonplace as Peter. What bothered me, when I first read the papers in *R.* v. *Durden*, was where and when I had heard it before. And then I remembered old cases, forgotten crimes and gang rivalry in a part of London to the east of Ludgate Circus in the days when I was making something of a name for myself as a defender at the Criminal Bar. These thoughts led me to remember Bill 'Knuckles' Huckersley, a heavyweight part-time boxer, full-time bouncer, and general factotum of a minicab organization in Bethnal Green. I had done him some service, such as getting his father off a charge of attempting to smuggle breaking-out instruments into Pentonville while Bill was detained there. This unlooked-for success moved him to send me a Christmas card every year and, as I kept his latest among my trophies, I had his address.

I thought he would be more likely to confide in me than in some professional investigator such as the admirable Fig Newton. Accordingly, I forsook Pommeroy's one evening after Court and made instead for the Black Spot pub in the Bethnal Green Road. There I sat staring moodily into a pint of Guinness as a bank of slot machines whirred and flashed and loud music filled a room, encrusted with faded gilt, which had become known, since a famous shooting had occurred there in its historic past, as the Luger and Lime Bar.

Knuckles arrived dead on time, a large, broad-shouldered man who seemed to move as lightly as an inflated balloon across the bar to where I sat. He pulled up a stool beside me and said, 'Mr Rumpole! This is an honour, sir. I told Dad you'd rang up for a meeting and he was over the moon about it. Eighty-nine now and still going. He sends his good wishes, of course.'

'Send him mine.' I bought Knuckles the Diet Coke and packet of curry-flavoured crisps he'd asked for and, as he crunched his way through them, the conversation turned to Doctor Petrus Wakefield. 'Petrus,' I reminded him. 'Not a name you'd forget. It seemed to turn up in a number of cases I did in my earlier years.'

'He treated friends of mine.' Knuckles lifted a fistful of crisps to his mouth and a sound emerged like an army marching through a field of dead bracken. 'They did get a few injuries in their line of business.'

'What do you mean by that, exactly?'

'Knife wounds. Bullet holes. Some of them I went around with used to attract those sort of complaints. You needed a doctor who wasn't going to get inquisitive.'

'And that was Doctor Petrus Wakefield?'

'He always gave you the first name, didn't he? Like he was proud of it. You got any further questions, Mr Rumpole? Don't they say that in Court?'

'Sometimes. Yes, I have. About Len Luxford. He used to come in here, didn't he?'

'The old Silencer? He certainly did. He's long gone, though. Got a window-cleaning business somewhere outside London.'

'Do you see him occasionally?'

'We keep in touch. Quite regular.'

'And he was a patient of Doctor Petrus?'

'We all were.'

'Anything else you can tell me about the Doctor?'

'Nothing much. Except that he was always on about acting. He wanted to get the boys in the nick into acting plays. I had it when I was in the Scrubs. He'd visit the place and start drama groups. I used to steer clear of them. Lot of dodgy blokes dressing up like females.'

'Did he ever try to teach Len Luxford acting?'

My source grinned, coughed, covered his mouth with a huge hand, gulped Diet Coke and said with a meaningful grin, 'Not till recently, I reckon.'

'You mean since they both lived at Chivering?'

'Something like that, yes. Last time I had a drink with Len he told me a bit about it.'

'What sort of acting are you talking about?' I tried not to show my feeling that my visit to the deafening Luger and Lime Bar was about to become a huge success, but Knuckles had a sudden attack of shyness.

'I can't tell you that, Mr Rumpole. I honestly can't remember.'

'Might you remember if we called you as a witness down the Old Bailey?'

My source was smiling as he answered, but for the first time since I'd known him his smile was seriously alarming. 'You try and get me as a witness down the Old Bailey and you'll never live to see me again. Not in this world you won't.'

After that I bought him another Diet Coke and then I left him. I'd got something out of Knuckles. Not very much, but something.

'This is one of those unhappy cases, Members of the Jury. One of those very rare cases when a member of the Police Force, in this case a very senior member of the Police Force, seems to have lost all his respect for the law and sets about to plot and plan an inexcusable and indeed a cruel crime.'

This was Marston Dawlish QC, a large, beefy man, much given to false smiles and unconvincing bonhomie, opening the case for the prosecution to an attentive Jury. On the Bench we had drawn the short straw in the person of the aptly named Mr Justice Graves. A pale, unsmiling figure with hollow cheeks and bony fingers, he sat with his eyes closed as though to shut out the painful vision of a dishonest senior copper.

'As I say, it is, happily, rare indeed to see a high-ranking police officer occupying that particular seat in an Old Bailey courtroom.' Here Marston Dawlish raised one of his ham-like hands and waved it in the general direction of the dock.

'A rotten apple.' The words came in a solemn, doom-laden voice from the Gravestone on the Bench.

'Indeed, your Lordship.' Marston Dawlish was only too ready to agree.

'We used to say that of police officers who might be less

than honest, Members of the Jury.' The Judge started to explain his doom-laden pronouncement. 'We used to call them "rotten apples" who might infect the whole barrel if they weren't rooted out.'

'Ballard!' This came out as a stentorian whisper at my leader's back. 'Aren't you going to point out that was an appalling thing for the Judge to say?'

'Quiet, Rumpole!' The Soapy Sam whisper was more controlled. 'I want to listen to the evidence.'

'We haven't got to the evidence yet. We haven't heard a word of evidence, but some sort of judicial decision seems to have come from the Bench. Get up on your hind legs and make a fuss about it!'

'Let me remind you, Rumpole, I'm leading counsel in this case. I make the decisions –'

'Mr Ballard!' Proceedings had been suspended while Soapy Sam and I discussed tactics. Now the old Gravestone interrupted us. 'Does your Junior wish to say something?'

'No, my Lord.' Ballard rose with a somewhat sickly smile. 'My Junior doesn't wish to say anything. If an objection has to be made, your Lordship can rely on me to make it.'

'I'm glad of that.' Graves let loose a small sigh of relief. 'I thought I saw Mr Rumpole growing restive.'

'I am restive, my Lord.' As Ballard sat down, I rose up like a black cloud after sunshine. 'Your Lordship seemed to be inviting the Jury to think of my client as a "rotten apple", as your Lordship so delicately phrased it, before we have heard a word of evidence against him.'

'Rumpole, sit down.' Ballard seemed to be in a state of panic.

'I wasn't referring to your client in particular, Mr Rumpole. I was merely describing unsatisfactory police officers in general.'

It was, I thought, a remarkably lame excuse. 'My Lord,' I

told him, 'there is only one police officer in the dock and he is completely innocent until he's proved guilty. He could reasonably object to any reference to "rotten apples" before this case has even begun.'

There was a heavy silence. I had turned to look at my client in the dock and I saw what I took to be a small, shadowy smile of gratitude. Ballard sat immobile, as though waiting for sentence of death to be pronounced against me.

'Members of the Jury,' Graves turned stiffly in the direction of the twelve honest citizens, 'you've heard what Mr Rumpole has to say and you will no doubt give it what weight you think fit.' There was a welcoming turn in the direction of the prosecution. 'Yes, Mr Marston Dawlish. Perhaps you may continue with your opening speech, now Mr Ballard's Junior has finished addressing the Court.'

Marston Dawlish finished his opening speech without, I was pleased to notice, any further support from the learned Judge. Doctor Petrus Wakefield was the first witness and he gave, I had to admit, an impressive performance. He was a tall, still, slender man with greying sideburns, slightly hooded eyes and a chin raised to show his handsome profile to the best possible advantage. When he took the oath he held the Bible up high and projected in a way which must have delighted the elderly and hard of hearing in the audience attending the Chivering Mummers. He smiled at the Jury, took care not to speak faster than the movements of the Judge's pencil, and asked for no special sympathy as a betrayed husband and potential murder victim. If he wasn't a truthful witness he clearly knew how to play the part.

An Old Bailey conference room had been reserved for us at lunchtime, so we could discuss strategy and eat sandwiches. Ballard, after having done nothing very much all morning, was tucking into a prawn and mayo when he looked up and met an outraged stare from Commander Durden.

'What the hell was that Judge up to?'

'Gerald Graves?' Ballard tried to sound casually unconcerned. 'Bit of an offputting manner, I agree. But he's sound, very sound. Isn't he, Rumpole?'

'Sound?' I said. 'It's the sound of a distant foghorn on a damp night.' I didn't want to depress the Commander, but he was depressed already, and distinctly angry.

'Whatever he sounds like, it seems he found me guilty in the first ten minutes.'

'You mean,' I couldn't help reminding the man of his denunciation of defence barristers, 'you found the Scales of Justice tipped towards the prosecution? I thought you said it was always the other way round.'

'I have to admit,' and the Commander spoke as though he meant it, 'I couldn't help admiring the way you stood up to this Judge, Mr Rumpole.'

'That was standing up to the Judge, was it?' I couldn't let the man get away with it. 'Not just another courtroom trick to get the Jury on our side and give the Scales of Justice a crafty shove?'

'I don't think we should discuss tactics in front of the client, Rumpole.' Soapy Sam was clearly feeling left out of the conversation. 'Although, I have to say, I don't think it was wise to attack the Judge at this stage of the case or indeed at all.' He'd got the last morsel of prawn and mayo sandwich on his chin and wiped it on a large white handkerchief before setting out to reassure the client. 'From now on, I shall be personally responsible for what is said in Court. As your leading counsel, I shall do my best to get back on better terms with Graves.'

'You mean,' the Commander looked distinctly cheated, 'he's going to get away with calling me a rotten apple?'

'I mean to concentrate our fire on this man Luxford. He's

got a string of previous convictions.' Ballard did his best to look dangerous, but it wasn't a great performance.

'First of all, someone's got to cross-examine the good Doctor Petrus Wakefield,' I reminded him.

'I shall be doing that, Rumpole. And I intend to do it very shortly. We don't want to be seen attacking the man whose wife our client unfortunately –'

'Rogered.' I was getting tired of Ballard's circumlocutions.

'Misconducted himself.' Ballard lowered his voice, and his nose, into a paper cup of coffee. This was clearly part of the case on which Soapy Sam didn't wish to dwell.

'You'll have to go into the whole affair,' I told him. 'It's provided the motive for the crime.'

'The alleged victim's a deceived husband.' Ballard shook his head. 'The Jury are going to have a good deal of sympathy for the Doctor.'

'If you ask him the questions I've suggested, they may not have all that much sympathy. You got my list, did you?'

I had given my learned leader ten good points for the cross-examination of Doctor Petrus. I had little faith in his putting them particularly clearly, or with more force and power of attack than he might have used if he'd been asking the Doctor if he'd driven up by way of the M25 or had his holiday yet. All the same, the relevant questions were written down, a recipe for a good cross-examination, and Ballard only had to lob them out across the crowded courtroom.

'I have read your list carefully, Rumpole,' my leader said, 'and quite frankly I don't think there's anything in it that it would be helpful to ask Doctor Wakefield.'

'It might be very helpful to the prosecution if you don't ask my questions.'

'I shall simply say "My client deeply regrets his unfortunate conduct with your wife" and sit down.'

'Sit down exhausted?' I couldn't help asking. 'Don't you want to get at the truth of this case?'

'Truth? My dear Rumpole,' Ballard was smiling, 'I didn't know you were interested in the truth. All these questions,' he lifted my carefully prepared list and dropped it on the table, 'seem nothing but a sort of smoke screen, irrelevant matter to confuse the Jury.'

'You read about my meeting with Knuckles Huckersley in the Black Spot pub?'

'I did, and I regretted the fact that a Member of the Bar would go to such lengths, or shall I say depths, to meet a potential witness.'

'You're not going to ask the Doctor about his practice in the East End?'

'I think the Jury would find that quite counter-productive. It could look like an attack on his character.'

'So you won't take the risk?'

'Certainly not.' Ballard's thoughts strayed back to his lunch. 'Are those sandwiches bacon and lettuce?'

'I rather imagine corned beef and chutney.' Mr Crozier, our instructing solicitor from Chivering, made a rare contribution to the discussion.

There was silence then. Ballard chewed his last sandwich in silence. No doubt I had broken every rule and shown a lamentable lack of faith in my learned leader, but I had to make the situation clear to our client, the copper who had shown his complete lack of faith in defending counsel.

'Well, Commander,' I said, 'you've got a barrister who's going to keep the scales tipped in what you said was the right direction.'

'Towards justice?' Bob Durden was trying to stick to his old convictions as a drowning man might to a straw.

'No,' I said. 'Towards a conviction. If it's the conviction of an innocent man, well, I suppose that's just bad luck and part of the system as you'd like it to work.'

There was a silence then, in the lunchtime conference room. Ballard was at ease in his position as the leader. No doubt I was being a nuisance, and breaking most of the rules, but he seemed to feel that he was still in charge and could demolish the corned beef and chutney in apparently contented silence. Mr Crozier looked embarrassed and the Commander was seriously anxious as he burst out, 'Are you saying, Mr Rumpole, that the questions you want asked could get me off?'

'At least leave you in with a chance.' I was prepared to promise him that.

'And Mr Ballard doesn't want to ask them?'

'I've told you. They'll only turn the Judge against us,' Ballard mumbled past the corned beef.

'And why do you want to ask them, Mr Rumpole?' The Commander was puzzled.

'Oh, I'm just one of those legal hacks you disapprove of,' I told him. 'I want you to walk out of Court laughing. I know that makes me a very dubious sort of lawyer, the kind you really hate, don't you, Commander Durden?'

In the silence that followed, our client looked round the room uncertainly. Then he made up his mind and barked out an order. 'I want Mr Rumpole's questions asked.'

'I told you,' Ballard put down his half-eaten sandwich, 'I'm in charge of this case and I don't intend to make any attack on the reputable Doctor whose wife you apparently seduced.'

'All right.' In spite of Ballard's assertion of his authority it was the Commander who was in charge. 'Then Mr Rumpole is going to have to ask the questions for you.'

I was sorry for Soapy Sam then, and I felt, I have to confess, a pang of guilt. He had behaved according to his fairly hopeless principles and could do no more. He rose to his feet, left his half-eaten sandwich to curl up on its plate, and spoke to his friend Mr Crozier who looked deeply embarrassed.

'Under the circumstances,' Ballard said, 'I must withdraw. My advice has not been taken and I must go. I can't say I expect a happy result for you, Commander, but I wish you well. I suppose you're not coming with me, Rumpole?'

As I say, I felt for the man, but I couldn't leave with him. Commander Durden had put his whole life in the hands of the sort of Old Bailey hack he had told the world could never be trusted not to pull a fast one.

'Doctor Wakefield, you're suggesting in this case that my client, Commander Durden, instigated a plan to kill you?'

'He did that, yes.'

'It wasn't a very successful plan, was it?'

'What do you mean?'

'Well, you're still here, aren't you? Alive and kicking.'

This got me a little stir of laughter from the Jury and a doom-laden warning from his Lordship.

'Mr Rumpole, for reasons which we need not go into here, your learned leader hasn't felt able to continue in this case.'

'Your Lordship is saying that he will be greatly missed?'

'I am saying no such thing. What I am saying is that I hope this defence will be conducted according to the high standard we have come to expect from Mr Ballard. Do I make myself clear?'

'Perfectly clear, my Lord. I'll do my best.' Here I was looking at the Jury. I didn't exactly wink, but I hoped they were prepared to join me in the anti-Graves society. 'Of course I can't promise anything.'

'Well, do your best, Mr Rumpole.' The old Gravestone

half closed his eyes as though expecting to be shocked by my next question. I didn't disappoint him.

'Doctor Wakefield, were you bitterly angry when you discovered that your wife had been sleeping with Commander Durden?'

'Mr Rumpole!' The Graves eyes opened again, but with no friendly expression. 'I'm sure the Jury will assume that Doctor Wakefield had the normal feelings of a betrayed husband.'

'I quite agree, my Lord. But the evidence might be more valuable if it came from the witness and not from your Lordship.' Before Graves could utter again, I launched another question at the good Doctor. 'Did you consider divorce?'

'I thought about it, but Judy and I decided to try to keep the marriage together for the sake of the children.'

'An admirable decision, if I may say so.' And I decided to say so before the doleful Graves could stir himself to congratulate the witness. 'You've produced the letter you found in your wife's handbag. By the way, do you make a practice of searching your wife's bag?'

'Only after I'd become suspicious. I'd heard rumours.'

'I see. So you found this letter, in which the Commander said they might be happier if you vanished from the face of the earth. Did you take that as a threat to kill you?'

'When I heard about the plot, yes.'

'When you heard about it from Luxford?'

'Yes.'

'But not at the time you found the letter?'

'It occurred to me it might be a threat, but I didn't believe that Bob Durden would actually do anything.'

'You didn't believe that?'

'No. But I thought he meant he wanted me dead.'

'And it made you angry?'

'Very angry.'

'So I suppose you went straight round to the Commander's office, or his house, and confronted him with it.'

'No, I didn't do that.'

'You didn't do that?' I was looking at the Jury now, in considerable surprise, with a slight frown and raised eyebrows, an expression which I saw reflected in some of their faces.

'May I ask why you didn't confront my client with his outrageous letter?'

'I didn't want to add to the scandal. Judy and I were going to try to make a life together.'

'That answer,' the sepulchral Graves' voice was now almost silky, 'does you great credit, if I may say so, Doctor Wakefield.'

'What may not do you quite so much credit, Doctor,' I tried to put my case as politely as possible, 'is the revenge you decided to take on your wife's lover. This letter,' I had it in my hand now and held it up for the Jury to see, 'gave you the idea. The ingenious revenge you planned would cause Bob Durden, and not you, to vanish. Isn't that the truth of the matter?'

'Are you suggesting, Mr Rumpole,' the Judge over-acted his astonishment, 'that we've all got this case the wrong way round and that it was Doctor Wakefield who was planning to murder your client?'

'Not murder him, my Lord. However angry the Doctor was, however deep his sense of humiliation, he stopped short of murder. No. What he planned for Mr Durden was a fate almost worse than death for a senior police officer. He planned to put him exactly where he is now, in the Old Bailey dock, faced with a most serious charge and with the prospect of a long term of confinement in prison.'

It was one of those rare moments in Court of absolute silence. The clerk sitting below the Judge stopped whispering into his telephone, no one came in or went out, opened a law book or sorted out their papers. The Jury looked startled at a new and extraordinary idea, everyone seemed to hold their breath, and I felt as though I had just dumped my money on an outside chance and the roulette wheel had started to spin.

'I really haven't the least idea what you mean.' Doctor Petrus Wakefield, in the witness box, looked amused rather than shaken, cheerfully tolerant at a barrister's desperate efforts to save his client, and perfectly capable of dealing with any question I might have the wit to ask.

Graves swooped to support the Doctor. 'Mr Rumpole, I presume you're going to explain that extraordinary suggestion.'

'Your Lordship's presumption is absolutely correct. I would invite your Lordship to listen carefully while I put my case to the witness. Doctor Wakefield,' I went on before Graves could summon his voice back from the depths, 'your case is that you learnt of the alleged plot to kill you when Luxford called to warn you. We haven't yet heard from Mr Luxford, but that's your story.'

'It's the truth.'

'Luxford warned you because he was grateful for the way you'd treated his mother?'

'That is so.'

'But you'd known Len Luxford, the Silencer as he was affectionately known by the regulars in the Black Spot in Bethnal Green, long before that, hadn't you?'

Doctor Wakefield took time to think. He must have thought of what the Silencer might say when he came to give evidence and he took a gamble on the truth. 'I had come across him. Yes.'

'Because you practised as a doctor in that part of London?'

'I did, yes.'

'And got to know quite a number of characters who lived on the windy side of the law?'

'It was my job to treat them medically. I didn't enquire into the way they lived their lives.'

'Of course, Doctor. Didn't some of your customers turn up having been stabbed, or with gunshot wounds?'

'They did, yes.' Once again the Doctor took a punt on the truth.

'So you treated them?'

'Yes. Just as you, Mr Rumpole, no doubt represented some of them in Court.'

It was a veritable hit, the Jury smiled, the Gravestone looked as though it was the first day of spring, and I had to beware of any temptation to underestimate the intelligence of Doctor Wakefield.

'Exactly so. And like me, you got to know some of them quite well. You got to know Luxford very well in those old days, didn't you?'

'He was a patient of mine.'

'You treated his wounds and kept quiet about them.'

'Probably.'

'Probably. So would it be right to say that you and the Silencer Luxford went back a long time, and he owed you a debt of gratitude?'

'Exactly!' The Doctor was pleased to agree. 'Which is why he told me about your client's plan to pay him to kill me.'

'I'm just coming to that. When you're not practising medicine, or patching up old gangsters, you spend a great deal of your time acting, don't you?'

'It's my great passion.' And here the Doctor's voice was projected and enriched. 'Acting can release us from ourselves. Call on us to create a new character.'

'Which is why you encouraged acting in prisons.'

'Exactly, Mr Rumpole! I'm glad you understand that, at least.'

There was a moment of rapport between myself and the witness, but I had to launch an attack which seemed, now that I was standing up in a crowded courtroom, like taking a jump in the dark off a very high cliff.

'I think you encouraged Len Luxford to act?'

'In the old days, when I did some work with prisoners, yes.'

'Oh, no, I mean quite recently. When you suggested he went for a chat with Commander Durden about police informers and came out acting the part of a contract killer.'

The Doctor's reaction was perfect: good-natured, half amused, completely unconcerned. 'I really have no idea what you're suggesting,' he said.

'Neither have I.' The learned Gravestone was delighted to join the queue of the mystified. 'Perhaps you'd be good enough to explain yourself, Mr Rumpole.'

'Certainly, my Lord.' I turned to the witness. 'It was finding the letter that gave you the idea, wasn't it? It could be used to support the idea that Commander Durden wanted you dead. You were going to get your revenge, not by killing him, nothing as brutally simple as that, but by getting him convicted of a conspiracy to murder you. By finishing his career, turning him into a criminal, landing him, the rotten apple in the barrel of decent coppers, in prison for a very long time indeed.'

'That is absolute nonsense.' The Doctor was as calm as ever, but I ploughed on, doing my best to sound more confident than I felt.

'All you needed was an actor for your small-cast play. So you got Len Luxford, who owed you for a number of favours, to act for you. All he had to do was to lie about what Commander

Durden had said to him when he arranged a meeting, and you thought that and the letter would be enough.'

'It's an interesting idea, Mr Rumpole. But of course it's completely untrue.'

'You're an excellent actor, aren't you, Doctor?' I took it slowly now, looking at the Jury. 'Didn't you have a great success in the Shakespeare play you did with the local Mummers?'

'I think we all did fairly well. What's that got to do with it?'

'Didn't you play Iago? A man who ruins his Commander by producing false evidence?'

'Mr Rumpole!' Graves' patience, fragile as it was, had clearly snapped at what he saw as my attempt to call a dead dramatist into the witness box. 'Have you no other evidence for the very serious suggestions you're making to this witness except for the fact that he played, who was it?' He searched among his notes. 'The man Iago?'

'Oh yes, my Lord.' I tried to answer with more confidence than I felt. 'I'd like the Jury to have a couple of documents.'

Mr Crozier had done his work well. Having surrendered Bob Durden's bank statements to the young man from the Crown Prosecution Service, he seemed to take it for granted that we should get Doctor Wakefield's in return. Now the Judge and the Jury had their copies, and I introduced the subject.

'Let me just remind you. Luxford saw Commander Durden on March the fifteenth. On March the twenty-first you went to Detective Inspector Mynot with your complaint that my client had asked Luxford to kill you for a payment of five thousand pounds, two and a half thousand down and the balance when the deed was done.'

'That's the truth. It's what I told the Inspector.'

'You're sure it's the truth?'

'I am on my oath.'

'So you are.' I looked at the Jury. 'Perhaps you could look at your bank statement. Did you draw out two and a half thousand pounds in cash on March the twenty-first? Quite a large sum, wasn't it? May I suggest what it was for?'

For the first time the Doctor missed his cue, looked about the Court as though hoping for a prompt, and, not getting one, invented. 'I think I had to pay . . . I seem to remember . . . Things were done to the house.'

'It wasn't anything to do with the house, was it? You were paying Len Luxford off in cash. Not for doing a murder, but for pretending to be part of a conspiracy to murder?'

The Doctor looked to Marston Dawlish for help, but no help came from that quarter. I asked the next question.

'When does he get the rest of the money? On the day Commander Durden's convicted?'

'Of course not!'

'Is that your answer?' I turned to the Judge. 'My Lord, may I just remind you and the Jury, there are no large amounts of cash to be seen coming out of Commander Durden's account during the relevant period.'

With that I sat down, and counsel for the prosecution suggested that as I had taken such an unconscionable time with Doctor Wakefield, perhaps the Court would rise for the day, and he would be calling Mr Luxford in the morning.

But he didn't call the Silencer the next morning or any other morning. I don't know whether it was the news of my cross-examination in the evening paper, or a message of warning from Knuckles, but in a fit of terminal stage fright Len failed to enter the Court. A visit by the police to the house from where he carried out his window-cleaning business only revealed a distraught wife, who had no idea where he had got to. I suppose he had enough experience of the law to understand that a charge of conspiracy to murder against the Commander might turn into a charge of attempting to pervert the course of justice against Doctor Wakefield and Len Luxford. So he went, with his cash, perhaps back to his old friends and his accustomed haunts, his one unsuccessful stab at the acting profession over.

When Marston Dawlish announced that without his vital witness the prosecution couldn't continue, Mr Justice Graves gave a heavy sigh and advised the twelve honest citizens.

'Members of the Jury, you have heard a lot of questions put by Mr Rumpole about the man – Iago. And other suggestions which may or may not have seemed to you to be relevant to this case. The simple fact of the matter is that the vital prosecution witness has gone missing – and Mr Marston Dawlish has asked me to direct you to return a verdict of "not guilty". It's an unfortunate situation, but there it is. So will your foreman please stand?'

I paid a last visit to the conference room to say goodbye to my client and Mr Crozier. The place had been cleaned up, ready to receive other sandwiches, other paper cups of coffee and other people in trouble.

'I suppose I should thank you.' The Commander was looking as confident again as he had on the telly. Only now he was smiling.

'I suppose you should thank me, the shifty old defence hack, and a couple of hard cases like Knuckles and Len Luxford. We doubtful characters saved your skin, Commander, and managed to tip the Scales of Justice in favour of the defence.'

'I shall go on protesting about that, of course.'

'I thought you might.'

'Not that I have any criticism of what you did in my case.

I'm sure you acted perfectly properly. You believed in my innocence.'

'No.' I had to say it, but I'm afraid it startled him. He looked shocked. His full lips shrank in disapproval, his forehead furrowed.

'You didn't believe in my innocence?'

'My belief is suspended. It's been left hanging up in the robing room for years. It's not my job to find you innocent or guilty. That's up to the Jury. All I can do is put your case as well as you would if you had,' and I said it in all modesty, 'anything approaching my ability.'

'I don't think I'd ever have thought up your attack on the Doctor,' he admitted.

'No, I don't believe you would.'

'So I'm grateful to you.'

It wasn't an over-generous compliment, but I said thank you.

'But you say you're not convinced of my innocence?' Clearly he could hardly believe it.

'Don't worry,' I told him. 'You're free now. You can go back to work.'

'That's true. I've been suspended for far too long.' He looked at his watch as though he expected to start immediately. 'It's been an interesting experience.' I was, I must say, surprised at the imperturbable Commander, who could fall passionately in love, wish an inconvenient husband off the face of the earth and call his own criminal trial merely 'interesting'. 'We live in different worlds, Mr Rumpole,' he told me, 'you and I.'

'So we do. You believe everyone who turns up in Court is guilty. I suspect some of them may be innocent.'

'You suspect, you say, but you never know, do you?'

And so he went with Mr Crozier. I fully expect to see

him again, in his impressive uniform, complaining from the television in the corner of our living-room about the Scales of Justice being constantly tipped in favour of the defence.

'You had a bit of luck in *R.* v. *Durden*.' Ballard caught me up in Ludgate Circus one afternoon when we were walking back from the Old Bailey. 'I gather Luxford went missing.'

'That's right,' I told him. 'Are you calling that luck?'

'Lucky for you, Rumpole. From what I read of your cross-examination, you were clearly irritating the Judge.'

'I'm afraid I was. I do have a talent for irritating judges.'

'Pity, that. Otherwise you are, in many ways, quite able.'

'Thank you, Ballard.'

'No, I should thank you for getting me out of that unpleasant case. Our clerk fixed me up with a rating appeal.'

'Good old Henry.'

'Yes, he has his uses. So you see I have a lot to thank you for, Rumpole.'

'You're entirely welcome, but will you promise me one thing?'

'What's that?'

'Please don't hug me, Ballard.'

'I told you, Rumpole, I could tell at once that there was something fishy about that client of yours.' Hilda's verdict on the Commander was written in stone.

'But he was acquitted.'

'You know perfectly well, Rumpole, that doesn't mean a thing. The next time he turns up on the telly I shall switch over to the other channel.'

Forget Graves, I thought, leave out Bullingham; you'd search for a long time down the Old Bailey before you found a Judge as remorseless and tough as She Who Must Be Obeyed!

Rumpole and the Right to Privacy

'Is no one, Rumpole, to be allowed to lead a private life any more? As I told them at my bridge club, they won't leave you alone. Everything has to get into the papers.'

'You mean we're to expect headlines in the tabloids: "Hilda Rumpole bids four hearts. Full story in the *Sun*"?'

'I know you like to make a joke of everything, but things are getting serious when I'm actually rung up by a journalist. He wanted to know all about you, Rumpole.'

'Really? What did he want to know?'

'More about the life of a well-known criminal barrister. What you did in your spare time, for instance.'

'Did you tell him I spent my evenings enjoying recreational drugs in the company of lap dancers?'

'Certainly not! I said it was absolutely no business of his, and you didn't want anything written about you in the papers. You don't, do you, Rumpole?'

Didn't I? I had, I'm afraid, felt a little thrill of pleasure as She Who Must uttered the words 'well-known criminal barrister'. It was not, of course, entirely unexpected. Since my resurrection and return to life and the law, and since my defence of Commander Durden, my fame had spread far beyond Equity Court and the Old Bailey, so I would not have objected forcefully to a well-written profile in some respectful broadsheet, headlined 'The Great Defender', no doubt with a photograph or mercifully drawn caricature. I could imagine the jealousy at the next Chambers meeting and Luci's gratitude for what I'd done for the 'image' of the Old Bailey hack.

'Well,' I started off cautiously, 'it might rather depend on how it was done.'

'It wouldn't depend on that at all, Rumpole. There are no circumstances in which I'd allow journalists into our mansion flat to notice our furniture and write about our knick-knacks. Privacy is sacred, Rumpole, I'm sure you'd agree.'

'Up to a point,' is what I might have said. But to save time, and for the avoidance of controversy, I kept it to 'You're quite right, Hilda.'

'Of course I'm right. Aren't there enough wars, I told him, and natural disasters, without you having to come worrying us for something to put in your paper?'

So not being a war or natural disaster, I reconciled myself to the status of a member of the newspaper-buying public who never gets profiled or caricatured or mentioned unless he becomes involved in a salacious scandal or features as the victim of violent crime. A few quotations in the reports when I was doing a particularly noteworthy case was all I could look forward to. The prospect of becoming Personality of the Week, 'Old Bailey Star Horace Rumpole', was best forgotten. Perhaps it was all for the best, and private life is something that should be cherished in secret, like a furtive love affair, or a miser's hoard of cash. No doubt Hilda was right and we didn't want our knick-knacks photographed. But, just sometimes, wasn't life like the law? It shouldn't only be lived but be seen to be lived.

These thoughts were uppermost in my mind at that moment, not only because of what Hilda told me, but because I had become involved in a case about the denial of human rights, and the protection of the privacy of a very rich man indeed. Sadly, I was not on the side of the big money brief in that case, nor was I the gallant defender of privacy. I was briefed by the *Chivering Argus* which had, in the circumstances set out in my instructions, played the unattractive and unsympathetic role of a Peeping Tom.

Sir Michael Smedley was to many people the ideal businessman, who had been able to pull himself up by what are still, in some relentlessly market-oriented circles, known as his bootstraps. (This phrase ignores the fact that no one except mountaineers and footballers wears boots nowadays or has any idea where the straps are kept.) Born into a family of old-fashioned union officials and shop stewards in Coventry, he devoted his time out of school to begging or buying old bicycles, repairing them expertly and selling them on at a small profit. In his teens he was doing the same thing with motorbikes and cars. By the time he was twenty, he'd opened a secondhand car business, which surpassed secondhand car businesses all over the Midlands. It was then, it seems, that he took a deep breath and surveyed the scene for a new field for his undoubted entrepreneurial skills.

He came to the conclusion that while the car industry might be in decline, going to bed at night was a habit never likely to go out of style. Accordingly, he took over some bankrupt motorworks for the manufacture of the first Smedley Slumberwell beds, which, helped on by some vaguely erotic advertising, became bestsellers in a mass of what had already become known as 'furniture outlets'. Mike Smedley was something of a celebrity, constantly in the news, calling on the government to do more to help business, and on schools to teach 'entrepreneurial skills' instead of such pointless subjects as the plays of Shakespeare or the causes of the Civil War. So he had, unlike Rumpole, appeared in the newspapers as Profile of the Week, done *Desert Island Discs* and various discussion programmes. He had, as he constantly told his listeners, no political affiliations; all he was anxious to do was to serve the public and make sure that as many of us as possible were tucked up safely at night in a Smedley Slumberwell superspring, shaped-to-your-body bed. His business career reached a peak when the government, faced with a rapidly increasing demand for beds in a number of new National Health hospitals, awarded the contract to Slumberwell in the face of stiff competition from other bed-makers. And there was no suggestion that the politically immaculate Sir Mike had made the smallest contribution to party funds.

None of the above, however, explains how I had come to be briefed by the *Chivering Argus* when the full force of the Smedley millions had been turned against it, following a writ alleging a breach of confidence and the invasion of Sir Mike's privacy by publishing a photograph of him on holiday in the Caribbean.

'Do you do human rights cases, Mr Rumpole?'

'All the time.'

I had immediately recognized the voice on the telephone as that of Crozier, the solicitor who had instructed Ballard and me, and finally me alone, in the defence of the Police Commander.

'I was deeply impressed by your handling of Bob Durden's case. He's very grateful, by the way. So when our local paper got a writ from Sir Michael's solicitors, I thought of you at once.'

'And you couldn't have thought of anyone better.' I was determined to give a passable imitation of someone who had the law of breach of confidence and the European Convention on Human Rights at their fingertips. 'These privacy cases can be tricky if not handled by someone experienced in that particular branch of the law.'

It turned out that Sir Mike was a local power in Chivering, having bought a large house just where the suburban spread met an area of comfortable and well-cultivated countryside. There he grew hedges, reclaimed ponds, produced organic crops and was generally regarded as a model landlord. He also bought up a chain of local newspapers which dealt with local weddings, funerals and garden fêtes and advertised, in many brightly coloured supplements, the extraordinary comfort of Smedley Slumberwell beds.

His one failure in the neighbourhood had been to buy the *Chivering Argus*, a paper edited by a member of the family that had founded it in the 1920s.

'I don't like him, Mr Rumpole. If you put me into the witness box I'll have to admit that I don't like Sir Mike at all. He's always either threatening to kill my paper with his competition or trying to bribe me to sell it to him. But we've got a loyal readership. Not a huge one, but loyal. So it's no use him trying to throw his weight about.'

If it ever came to a physical encounter Mr Rankin, the editor, would have very little weight to throw. He was a small, bird-like man, with bright eyes and a head cocked to one side, who sat up very straight with his arms folded as though he had just fluttered down and alighted on the edge of my client's chair. He had been brought to my room in Chambers by the ecclesiastical-looking Crozier, sniffed around the place in a mood of apparent excitement, asked for the history of the mementoes of old murder trials, and when I had satisfied his curiosity, started to talk about his case as though a hefty claim for damages was no more serious that a slight sniffle or an irritating draught.

'That's why we published the photograph. Just a bit of

mischief. I'll freely admit that. Our way of getting our own back, or what have you. Just so our readers could have a giggle at Sir High and Mighty Mike, the local celebrity who thinks everything's for sale.'

'You're saying you published the photograph just to get a laugh?' I was beginning to get the message. The editor was going to prove a highly unsatisfactory witness. Not only his sense of humour but his language seemed to have come out of some long-defunct boys' comic. 'Just a July jape, you see, Mr Rumpole. And then, ouch! We're landed with this writ.'

'You say your nephew took the photograph?'

'Certainly. Young Jim. He'd gone to the Caribbean in his gap year, after school.'

'And Sir Michael has a holiday home in St Lucia,' Crozier reminded me.

'Of course,' I told him, 'I'd've expected nothing less.'

'Jim was working in the Sugar and Spice Bar when the Great Big Cheese himself took the whole place over for a party with his chums.'

'A *private* party, Mr Rumpole. And he made the management sign a contract – no photographs, no press, no divulging of the guest list . . . They agreed to complete confidentiality.' Crozier seemed to take some sort of gloomy delight in the difficulties of the case.

'Of course, no one realized Jim knew all about Sir Mike, and that he had his camera with him.'

'The young man was interested in taking pictures of wildlife on the island,' Crozier filled in the details.

'So he was all prepared to photograph wildlife in the Sugar and Spice Bar?' I asked.

'He thought it a great wheeze and managed very cleverly.' Rankin seemed understandably proud of his nephew. 'Of course, it was quite late and the party had been going on some time and they'd all had a skinful. And they'd fixed up a sort of swirling light over the dancers, so no one noticed the flash.'

'And young Jim,' I felt I had to ask the pertinent question, 'apart from his talent for snapping local fauna, did he know that the management had signed a contract, no photographs allowed?'

'Oh, he knew that.' The editor was smiling happily. 'But he did it as a prank. He knew how much his picture would delight his old uncle.'

'And as a prank his old uncle published this picture in his paper?'

'You've got it, Mr Rumpole.' Rankin was delighted. 'How could I resist the temptation?'

'I really don't know. But if you could have you might have saved yourself an action for breach of confidentiality, invasion of privacy and all the trimmings.'

I picked up the photograph and looked at it again, but it had got no better. Sir Michael Smedley, the great business tycoon, was a large, beefy-looking individual, with his hair brushed forward as though surrounding a monk's tonsure. He was grinning happily and strutting in some sort of celebratory dance, clearly enjoying his private party. His dancing partner, whom I took to be a darkly beautiful local girl, was dancing with much finger-snapping and flashing of white teeth. She was naked from the waist up and her sizeable brassiere, in that golden moment immortalized by young Jim's camera, was draped about Sir Michael Smedley's ears.

'Rumpole, I hear you're doing an invasion of privacy case.'

'Breach of confidence. Invasion of privacy. Outrageous infringement of human rights. Yes, Claude. That's the sort of practice I carry on these days. I've left the petty larcenies and the public-bar affrays to Old Bailey hacks like you.' I didn't tell Erskine-Brown that I had been briefed by the *Chivering Argus* because the paper now faced bankruptcy as a result of Sir Mike's charge and couldn't afford a fashionable silk, or that, so far as I could see at the moment, there was little or no defence to the tycoon's deadly writ.

'I assume,' Erskine-Brown had come into my room wearing what was, even for him, a peculiarly doleful expression, 'that you know quite a bit by now of the law concerning the invasion of privacy?'

'I have that at my fingertips,' I assured him. 'Is there anything wrong with your privacy, Claude?'

'It has, I'm afraid, Rumpole, been seriously invaded.' With which he sank into my client's chair, no longer a reasonably confident Q C, but a man like any other, in desperate need of reassuring legal advice. 'I came to you as an expert in this class of case.'

'Then you've come to the right man, Claude. So fire away. What's the problem?'

'The problem, Rumpole, is, I'm very much afraid, Mercy Grandison.'

I considered the matter for a while, and then I asked what seemed to me to be an essential question. 'Who the hell is Mercy Grandison?'

'Rumpole, I can't believe it!'

'You can't believe what?'

'That you don't know who Mercy Grandison is.'

'I don't.'

'You've never watched *Shopping Mall*?'

'Never.'

'She's the one who runs the Boutique at the end of the Mall. You know, the one who broke up her marriage with Barry from the Sock Shop and had such a ghastly time with Bertrand from the Bistro des Voyageurs.'

'Enormously interesting, Claude. But how does any of that threaten your privacy?'

'*Shopping Mall* doesn't, but Mercy Grandison does.'

'An actress?'

'And author. That's the terrible thing, Rumpole. She's got a book coming out next month. It's been advertised in the *Telegraph*.'

'A history of shopping?'

'Unfortunately not. It's her life story – *A Wandering Star*. "How Mercy Grandison, born Mary Grimes, sixth daughter of a Wisbech plumber, rose to become Queen of the Soaps. In this touching memoir, Mercy reveals the heartbreaks behind the glitter of show business."' Erskine-Brown had pulled a crumpled cutting from his wallet and put it, I thought reverently, on my desk. I had to confess I still didn't see what the bothered QC was worrying about.

'She reveals the heartbreaks, Rumpole.'

'What's that got to do with you?'

There was a pause, during which a certain amount of wrestling for the soul of Erskine-Brown seemed to be taking place. When the struggle was over he allowed himself to speak. 'I'd better confess to you, Rumpole.'

'You probably should, if you want my advice.'

'It was years ago. I'd gone up to Grimsby to do a lengthy fraud.'

'That's forgivable.'

'And one evening I went to the threatre. The local Rep. I went to see *Private Lives* by Noel Coward. A young girl in a white dress came out on a moonlit balcony.'

'In Grimsby?'

'No, the South of France! I was just totally knocked out, Rumpole. Stunned, I suppose . . . I made a complete fool of myself. I waited for her at the stage door. We went out for supper every night for the rest of the week. In the end, I asked her back to the Trusthouse. I'm telling you all this because I need your help desperately. She told me she thought I was "rather sweet".'

'There's no accounting for tastes' is what I might have said, but I didn't. Instead I asked, 'So what happened exactly?'

'*It* happened.'

'It?'

'Yes, *it*. I have to tell you, Rumpole, it was one of the most important things in my life! The next morning we said goodbye on Grimsby Station. But I still think about it. When there's nothing in Court, and Philly's away on circuit, or when life seems completely uneventful, I think about her, Rumpole. I get a great deal of quiet pleasure from thinking about Mercy. And I'm very sure you'd do the same.'

'I take it you met her from time to time, after your night in the Trusthouse?'

'Never again, Rumpole. Not ever.' The fellow had returned to his memories as though he had left me to take a bath. He was luxuriating in the warm water of his past, and I only got snatches of it, reminiscences through the bathroom door.

'So it was a last goodbye?'

'I'll never forget it. On Grimsby Station. You see, I had just got married to Philly. It was a long time ago, of course, before we had the children . . .'

'And the learned Judge knows nothing about it?'

'Nothing, Rumpole. But she's going to find out when Mercy's book is serialized in the *Daily Post*, which Philly demolishes at breakfast.'

'And you don't think she'll be best pleased?'

'So soon after we were married? She'll bring it up every time we have an argument. She'll tell me she can never trust me again. She'll . . .' Here his small store of language seemed to have run out. 'She'll never let me forget it, Rumpole.'

'Even though she had a walk-out with that appalling MP?'

'That'll be my fault too, if she finds out. What can I do, Rumpole? It's my private life. How can I protect myself?'

'Well, of course, when you parted on Grimsby Station . . .'

'Yes, yes, tell me!' The drowning man clutched eagerly at a straw. 'Give me your opinion.'

'. . . You obviously asked her to sign a solemn undertaking promising never verbally, or in writing, or by any form of technical communication which might be invented in the future, to divulge to anyone, or to any device, the events which had occurred between you and the soap star in the Trusthouse Forte hotel. No doubt you had such a document prepared. Did you get her to sign it in front of witnesses?'

'Don't be ridiculous, Rumpole. Of course I didn't.'

'Then I'm afraid your legal position is distinctly dicey. Not to put too fine a point on it, Claude, I would say you were up shit creek and deprived of a paddle. No case of breach of confidence. Look here, are you sure she's written about it? Have you read it?'

'It's not out yet. I told you. But of course she's written about Grimsby. It was one of the greatest moments of our lives. Do you think I'd be right to tell Philly? Should I warn her?'

'Don't jump,' I reminded him of an old legal maxim, 'before you get to the stile. The world is full of nervous husbands leaping about in level fields thinking they've got to clear obstructions which aren't there. I suppose it might be possible to keep the story in question out of Dame Phillida's paper.'

'Oh, Rumpole, would you do this for me? As my legal adviser would you try? They'll listen to you, now you're briefed in the great Sir Michael's privacy case.'

> Good name in man and woman, dear my lord,
> Is the immediate jewel of their souls:
> Who steals my purse steals trash; 'tis something, nothing;
> T'was mine, 'tis his, and has been slave to thousands:
> But he that filches from me my good name
> Robs me of that which not enriches him,
> And makes me poor indeed.

These words, spoken by him whom Mr Justice Graves called 'The man Iago', ran through my mind as I took the short walk from Equity Court to Pommeroy's Wine Bar. Fleet Street was crowded with people leaving work, waiting in bus queues or hurrying to the tube station. There were secretaries laughing together, last-minute shoppers, men taking arms to steer each other into the pub opposite the Law Courts. Soft, misty rain was falling, so the newspaper seller under the archway into the Temple was covering up his male-interest magazines with plastic sheets. I looked into so many faces and wondered what secrets lay hidden, what private acts or memories called out for protection. Unwise love affairs, probably, small dishonesties, perhaps, minor betrayals, without a doubt, but I didn't imagine many private lives featured murder, treason or other serious crimes. And then I wondered how many of the men scurrying for the train, or back-slapping their way into saloon bars, would be seriously upset by the publication of a photograph of themselves with a bra around their ears. There would, after all, be nothing much they could do about it. Breach of confidence cases for the protection of privacy are a luxury reserved for the rich. You'd have to be as well heeled as Sir Mike before you could bring a case.

The words of Iago and accompanying thoughts had brought me to the door of Pommeroy's, and as I stepped up to it there was a small flash of light in the surrounding damp-

Rumpole and the Right to Privacy

ness and I saw a girl with red hair, wearing a blue anorak, point a camera at me. Was I to be snapped like a starlet arriving at a film premiere? Was tomorrow's headline going to be 'Horace Rumpole arrives at Pommeroy's Wine Bar'? It was all extremely puzzling, but as the girl closed her camera and hurried away, and as I moved rapidly towards my first glass of Château Thames Embankment, I thought no more about it.

I had taken my bottle of just tolerable claret to a table in a corner of Pommeroy's, and was flicking through the *Evening Standard*, which seemed short of any article entitled 'Horace Rumpole: is he the Greatest Living Defender?', when I saw Liz Probert downing a vodka in the company of Mervyn Lockward, Queer Customer, a tall, languid, human-rights barrister, who occupied alternative Chambers in the Euston Road and refused, on principle, to appear for landlords, police officers and employers or any male person accused of a sexual offence. He seemed, as usual, delighted to find himself in his own company and was looking down his nose at Liz with the sort of patronizing smile which he wore, sometimes with fatal results, when addressing juries. In the course of time, he gave her a light kiss on the forehead and glided off, no doubt to enjoy the vegetarian alternative at a dinner of the anti-globalization society, where he would be booked to make a speech.

When he had gone, Liz joined me with a heavy sigh. 'Isn't Mervyn a wonderful barrister?'

'If that's your idea of being a barrister.' I was, I have to confess, less than enthusiastic. 'He's not an old taxi cab like me. More like a hired car only available to travel on certain routes for a certain class of person.' I saw her face fall a couple of inches so, by way of causing a diversion, I asked, 'Do you have any secrets you want to keep hidden, Liz?'

The look of vague disappointment turned to nothing less than panic. 'Rumpole!' Her voice had sunk to a whisper. 'You've found out!'

'Found out what?'

'You promise you won't tell Mervyn?'

'Of course not, if you don't want me to . . . It's just that I was wondering – I mean, hasn't everyone?'

'What?'

'Something they want to keep private.'

'With good reason!'

'Probably. But as for you, Liz, I can't believe . . .'

'Don't you think I'm ashamed of it, Rumpole? Horribly ashamed.'

'I'm sure there's no need.'

'Yes, there is a need. You know very well there's a need. All I can say is, I was very young and silly at the time.'

'Then I'm sure it was nothing serious.'

'Of course it was serious! I'm not saying it wasn't serious. It's just that, well, I had these Old Labour parents. They went on Ban the Bomb marches. They spent nights outside the South African Embassy singing "We shall overcome". It's natural to revolt when you're young. You must have felt that too, Rumpole.'

'I think I've felt like revolting all my life.'

'There you are then, you see? But mine was a one-off. An act of immature defiance. I'm ashamed of it, I really am.'

'What was it you're ashamed of? Just remind me.' By now my curiosity was thoroughly aroused.

'It was my first term at Uni.'

'Yes, of course . . .'

I waited for a fascinating revelation from the Probert past. All I got was, 'I joined the Conservative Association!'

'Oh dear!' I did my best to look suitably shocked.

'It was only for a term. Then I came to my senses. Oh, Rumpole! Give me your solemn promise you won't tell Mervyn.'

'I promise, solemnly.'

'Thank you, Rumpole.' Enormously relieved, so it seemed, Liz planted a kiss, which landed slightly to the left of my nose. Looking up from this experience, I saw the red-headed girl in the anorak standing at the bar and looking across at us with considerable interest.

A week later, I was surprised to get, in Chambers, a telephone call from someone called Gervase Johnson. He invited me, most unexpectedly, to the fashionable Myrtle restaurant in Long Acre for 'a chat over a few glasses of bubbles'. He was, I was delighted to learn, working on a profile of 'Horace Rumpole, Counsel for the Defence' for the *Daily Fortress*.

Before I could bask in the limelight of the Gervase Johnson interview, however, I had another call, which took me to the Chambers of Hugo Winterton, leading counsel for Sir Michael Smedley and the appointed protector of his privacy.

'Bit of a change for you, isn't it, Rumpole, civilized litigation in the Law Courts after the rough and tumble of the Old Bailey?'

'If you call it civilized, hopping about with some girl's bra round your ears . . .' I was, I have to confess, stung by the man's reference to the Courts where the Great Defender carried on his practice.

'He was relaxing, Rumpole. I expect you relax yourself when you're on holiday, don't you?'

'Not by prancing about decorated by my wife Hilda's underwear.' Then I asked why he'd called for the pleasure of my company.

'I thought we might knock our clients' heads together, you

and I, Rumpole. No need for a prolonged fight about this, is there? I'm sure we could find a fairly painless way out, between us?'

What was wrong with Hugo Winterton was that there was nothing wrong with him. His smile, unlike that of Liz Probert's hero, was neither aloof nor patronizing. He was good looking, middle-aged, and the excellent coffee served in his Chambers came in solid porcelain mugs. His handsome, amused wife smiled on me from the photograph frame on his desk, and so did two fair-haired and charming children. His Chippendale chairs, his old 'Spy' cartoons of vanished judges, the blue vase of white tulips, his bright and clearly enthusiastic Junior – Imogen, as he introduced her – all these seemed to have been carefully selected by a QC determined never to put a foot wrong. He even pushed a mother of pearl box containing small cigars towards me.

'Your clerk told us you use these. Please, do light up. Imogen and I have absolutely no objection in the world to people smoking.'

Was I being led gently into some ambush? Probably. However, I couldn't resist the temptation, and I sent a small smoke ring hovering over Hugo Winterton's tulips.

'Naturally, Mike was very upset when your little paper published the picture. All right, he was making a bit of a fool of himself, but we've all got to let our hair down sometimes. What he doesn't want is to have the picture popping up in every blessed newspaper. So he's got to appear to win this case.'

' "Appear to"?'

'Afraid so. And win so convincingly it's going to scare off all the other members of our sex-starved, scandal-loving press. So there's got to be an order for a phenomenal amount of damages.'

'How much?'

'We were thinking in terms of a quarter of a million – just as a warning to others.'

'Well, I'd better be going.' I started to prise my body from the chair. 'Thanks for the cheroot.'

'No, wait a minute.' Winterton was still smiling. 'Just between ourselves, I believe I could persuade Mike not to enforce the order. I doubt if either your paper or the editor's got the money. Your client will only pay his own costs, and of course Mike would want some permanent editorial control over the *Argus*.'

'You mean he wants to take it over?'

'Just to see it doesn't make any more unprovoked attacks on him.'

'And advertise his beds.'

'That might be part of it, of course.'

'And this order for a quarter of a million damages?'

'That would stay in the background.'

'To be enforced at any time, if my client doesn't give Sir Mike exactly what he orders.'

'It's a possibility, of course. We'd hope it wouldn't come to that.'

'A pious hope!'

'So, do you think we might do business, along these lines?' It was all extremely polite. Hugo Winterton seemed genuinely anxious to come to what he thought was a painless solution.

However, during the last few weeks I had read all the cuttings, a huge collection, sent to me by Crozier about the life, business dealings and matrimonial history of Sir Mike. I had also looked in vain for his political affiliations, without success. All I got were statements that he had no interest in politicians or politics and that the way he voted was entirely his own affair. I couldn't say that I had found a golden key to unlock all Sir Mike's secrets, but I had thought of a possible line of attack, and I wasn't about to surrender to Winterton without further argument.

'I'll put it to the editor,' I promised my learned opponent. 'But he's a pretty tough sort of a character.' I gave my preferred vision of the bird-like Rankin. 'I'm not sure he'd agree to being in Sir Mike's pocket for the indefinite future.'

'Do your best with him, Rumpole, my dear old fellow. We don't want to have to waste our time preparing for a fight, do we?'

'I'm not too worried about that.' Perhaps I should have reminded him that I was on my way to an interview to be entitled, when it was published, 'Rumpole: the Great Defender.'

'One. Two. Three. Four. Testing . . . testing . . . testing. Work, you little bugger! Work!'

The recording device lay ready to receive Rumpole's message to the world. It was a reluctant participant in the interview, however. Sometimes its red light glowed for a while, but then it faded and a blow from the interviewer's heavy fist failed to revive it. In the end, Gervase Johnson picked up a notebook and announced that he was going to do it the old-fashioned way. He was, I thought, an old-fashioned brand of journalist, with buttons straining across a sizeable stomach, white hair falling over his ears and the sort of patient smile that seemed prepared to live through any determined rebuff or casual humiliation.

Around us the crowd of faces, half-remembered from the gossip columns or Hilda's favourite soaps, chattered, called to each other, blew kisses, or gave interviews out to obedient machines. I had talked my way through the Japanese sushi starter and we were well into the seared monkfish with tomato coulis, with only a fleeting longing for mashed potatoes and steak and kidney pudding. I had given Gervase Johnson a résumé of my famous cases, dwelt at length on the turning point in my career (when I did the Penge Bungalow Affair alone and without a leader). I had given him classic examples of how a working knowledge of bloodstains, or signs of uncertainty in handwriting, can win a difficult case, when I began to notice that his hand was moving ever more slowly across the notebook page and the grasped pencil seemed to be giving up work. By the time I had reached my account of the mysterious case of the disappearing juror, the moving hand had stopped completely and no more notes were taken.

'I think what our readers will be interested in, Mr Rumpole,' here Gervase took a refreshing swig of the New Zealand Sauvignon the waiter had recommended, 'is how a busy barrister unwinds. Living on your nerves, aren't you? Will you give us an insight into your private life?'

'Certainly.'

'That's very generous of you.' Gervase gripped the pencil with renewed enthusiasm. 'I know some people don't like talking about that sort of thing.'

'Oh, I don't mind at all.'

'Good for you. Carry on, Mr Rumpole.'

'When the day's work is done –'

'And you feel the need to relax completely?'

'Exactly. I get outside, let's say, half a bottle of Pommeroy's Very Ordinary . . .'

'With a charming young companion?'

'With a private detective, or my friendly solicitor Bonny Bernard, or some more than usually disappointed member of Chambers.'

'You're a lucky man, Mr Rumpole.'

'In some ways.'

'The story is you were seen being kissed by a particularly attractive young lady in the wine bar.'

'Liz Probert?' I looked at the man with mild surprise. 'How do you know that?'

'Oh, we've been making a few enquiries. We've had a photographer out after you. Material for the article. I suppose you're not going to tell me how you spent the rest of the evening?'

'Certainly. I went back to my flat in the Gloucester Road. I had supper with my wife in the kitchen. A chop, I think. And baked jam roll. We watched the ten o'clock news and went to bed early. That is my private life.' I have to admit, I was growing impatient with this journalist who didn't seem to be interested in bloodstains. 'There's your story. Make what you like of it. I'm not Sir Mike Smedley. I don't want to sue anyone for writing about how I spend my evenings.'

'Sir Michael.' Gervase spoke in tones of awe and wonder. 'Is he a great man, Mr Rumpole? You're going to have a tough job cross-examining him.'

'Oh, I don't know.' I wasn't going to admit the possibility of defeat. 'Perhaps I'll think of something. He must have a weak spot, a chink in his armour?'

'Everyone's tried to find one, but he's clean as a whistle. The tabloids tried to pin something on him when he landed that contract for NHS beds.'

'I read something about that. Wasn't there a suggestion he'd done a deal with Gerry Hindle about a huge secret subsidy to Party coffers? Wasn't that the story?'

'Which collapsed as soon as it was mentioned. Sir Michael didn't even sue for damages.'

'Unusual.'

'He told me all about it when I interviewed him. The truth was, he said, he'd never spoken to Lord Hindle. Never even met him. He's not the sort to fraternize with politicians. Any more than you are, I should imagine, Mr Rumpole. I'm sure you prefer the company of attractive young lady barristers like Miss Probert, for instance.'

'I'm sorry to disappoint you,' I told him. 'But like the tabloids over the bed deal you've got the story completely wrong. Stick to the Penge Bungalow Murders. The readers of the *Daily Fortress* are going to find that far more interesting than my non-existent romances.'

At which the resigned journalist hit his little machine again, and when, to his amazement, the red light glowed steadily, recorded with a sigh of resignation some of my more sensational cases, while I refreshed my memory with another bottle of the New Zealand white.

Afterwards, I discovered that having a profile written for the papers was rather more irritating than not having a profile written for the papers. I bought the *Daily Fortress* every morning at the tube station and turned the pages nervously, dreading a description of my latest 'squeeze' being the personable Liz Probert, who would then berate me furiously for treating her as a trophy mistress and intruding on her privacy. I wondered if I should warn her, but remembering what I had told Claude about jumping stiles I put it off, and gradually I looked less eagerly and far less often into the pages of the *Daily Fortress*.

'Thank you for your advice, Rumpole. I'm so glad I didn't take it.'

Claude Erskine-Brown had come into my room just as I was trying, with diminishing success, to think of a reasonable defence in the case of *Smedley* v. *The Chivering Argus*.

'Which advice was that, Erskine-Brown?' I scarcely looked up from my brief.

'You advised me not to tell Philly about Mercy the actress. You said I shouldn't jump before I got to the stile. Well, I jumped, Rumpole. I leaped high up in the air and it's been a huge success. She doesn't mind at all.'

'You told her about Grimsby?'

'I did. And she said she would read Mercy's book with interest. She was truly glad I'd had such a romantic past. Quite frankly, she said, she'd never have believed me capable of a great passion. It also made her feel much better about her recent fling with that Conservative MP you defended. Of course, that's all over, and –'

'Well, that's fine!' Being busily engaged, I stopped Claude in mid flow. 'I'm so glad everything's back to normal in the Erskine-Brown home. Of course, you never know how wives are going to take things, but it must be a considerable weight off your mind.'

'Considerable. But isn't it extraordinary . . .'

'I'm sorry. I've got my privacy and breach of confidentiality starting next week.'

'Philly's trying that one. She thinks it's absolutely terrible that your newspaper should publish pictures of him at a private party. She's going to give you a rough ride, Rumpole.'

'Thank you,' I said, 'for those few kind words.' But by then he had drifted off and left me.

I had, of course, told Rankin the editor about Hugo Winterton's offer. I explained that the order for heavy damages wouldn't be enforced, provided he didn't do anything else to annoy the great Sir Mike, and I asked what our answer should be.

'Tell him, Mr Rumpole,' the editor's head was on one side as he pecked away at a suitable response, 'to save his breath to cool his porridge.' It was a long time since I had heard that expression and I couldn't help admiring the spirit it showed. 'So we're going to go on with the dance, Mr Rumpole. What japes!'

It would all have been more fun, I thought, had I been able to think of an arguable defence.

So when I rose in the unfamiliar terrain of Queen's Bench Court Four to mount an attack on Sir Mike, I found myself perilously short of ammunition.

I had walked up from Equity Court to that pinnacled château, the Law Courts in the Strand, and crossed the great mosaic floor (where in the evenings, Erskine-Brown assured me with a wistful sigh, girl secretaries came out to play badminton) to a strange robing room where alien barristers, practising civil law, were chattering in low, respectful voices about contracts and charter parties and negotiable instruments instead of laughing at fraud, robbery and sudden death. A strange race who, as that old darling Alfred Lord Tennyson said, 'hoard, and sleep, and feed, and know not me'.

All through Hugo Winterton's opening and the undisputed evidence of the agreement about the private party, I was trying to think of questions. And then Sir Mike entered the witness box, where he stood, big, broad-shouldered, with a determinedly youthful haircut, and gave his evidence in a Brummie accent which announced that, in spite of all his wealth and outspoken opinions about everything under the sun, he was, above all, a man of the people.

And as soon as he arrived and opened his mouth for the first time I saw, with a sinking of the heart, that the learned Judge Dame Phillida Erskine-Brown was smiling at him. Of course, I should have known it. He was just her type: forthright, perfectly satisfied with himself and determinedly masculine – a complete contrast, it has to be admitted, to the Judge's well-meaning, opera-loving and frequently confused husband.

Phillida's affection for the witness was not of the same flagrantly sexual order as that flaunted by Judge Bullingham for the Mrs Fagin of the London Underground. But she greeted too many of his answers with little nods of approval and smiled when she made a careful note of what he had said. I also noticed that, when at last I rose to cross-examine, my former pupil, whom I'd always thought of as a friend and ally, had a stare of judicial severity for Rumpole. I allowed myself an extra-long pause before the first question, hoping that this might disconcert our confident witness, but after less than ten seconds the Judge put in her oar.

'Mr Rumpole, if you have any questions this is the time to start asking them.'

This got a broad grin from Sir Mike, and from me an elaborately polite 'I'm so grateful to your Ladyship for reminding me of the elements of Court procedure. I can assure your Ladyship I haven't forgotten what I'm here for.' Then I turned to the witness. 'Sir Michael, are you thoroughly ashamed of what you did that evening at the Sugar and Spice Bar in St Lucia?'

'No, Mr Rumpole. I'm not at all ashamed.'

'You were capering around with a topless dancer, wearing her brassiere as ear muffs.'

'That is what the picture shows. Yes.'

'You're not in the least ashamed of having done that?'

'It was all good clean fun. It was in the spirit of the party.'

'Was it? Were many of your guests wearing bras round their heads?'

'Not that I noticed.' Sir Mike's answer, not my question, got a smile from the Judge, and a ripple of laughter from his legal team.

'If they had been, you would have seen nothing wrong with it?'

'Harmless fun, Mr Rumpole.'

'Just an expression of the party spirit?'

'He has told us that.' Her Ladyship gave me the small, sharp sigh that meant 'For God's sake, get on with it.'

'Yes, my Lady. But he hasn't told us this. If it was all just clean fun and nothing to be ashamed of, what's wrong with everyone who happens to read the *Chivering Argus* enjoying this photograph?'

'It was a private party,' said Sir Mike.

'It may or may not have been. But even if it was, why on earth have you trundled out this great legal sledgehammer to crack this perfectly harmless little photograph?'

'Some people, Mr Rumpole,' and here Phillida went too far, in my opinion, in lending a hand to a far-from-helpless witness, 'value their privacy.'

'I suppose you'll be grateful to accept the answer her Ladyship has offered you?'

Phillida was about to protest when I said that, but was wise enough to sit quietly. Sir Mike showed his gratitude to her.

'I do value my privacy. Yes.'

'I thought you'd say that. So does it come to this? If the *Argus* had just published a picture of you drinking a cup of tea at this party you'd have sued them for enormous damages?'

'Because I value my privacy, yes.'

'Let's see how much you really value it.' I began to burrow in the huge pile of press cuttings Rankin had provided. 'You've given, by my count, at least fifty interviews on radio, television and to various papers about yourself, your life, your career and your views on everything, from asylum seekers and one-parent families to homosexual marriage and the Euro. Is that correct?'

'I've been asked my opinion quite often, yes.'

'And given it, with a great deal of information about yourself?'

'When it was appropriate.'

'"When it was appropriate"?' I repeated his words and found myself turning to look at the Jury box, which I should have remembered was empty, the trial being entirely in the hands of Dame Phillida, the learned Judge. 'You found it "appropriate" when you had to deal with intimate details of your private life, didn't you?'

'I don't think so.' Sir Mike was, I thought, unwise to argue the point.

'How many times have you been married?'

'Is that a relevant question?' The Judge was back in the arena.

'If your Ladyship will listen patiently,' I ventured on a mild rebuke, 'the relevance will become obvious.' I might have added 'even to your Ladyship', but I thought better of it.

'When your first marriage ended, did you give an interview to the *Daily Post* printed under the headline "Heartbreak when I broke up with Danielle"?'

'I didn't write the headline, Mr Rumpole.'

'I know you didn't. But did you say this: "Sexually, I believed Danielle and I were perfectly suited. She left because she found the lifestyle of the lead singer of a rock band suited her tastes more than the quiet and secure home and life I had provided." Did you say that for publication in a tabloid with a huge circulation?'

'I may have said something like it.'

'Something very like it. And then we get "How I've found true happiness with Susan". Susan was your second wife?'

'She was, yes.'

'Sadly, four or five years later we get another interview: "Money and worldly success are no compensation for a broken heart". Did you give that interview?'

'I think so, yes.'

'Well, I can only wish you better luck the third time around.'

'I don't see what my marriages have to do with this case.'

'I have to say, Mr Rumpole,' Dame Phillida chimed in again, 'neither do I.'

'Then let me enlighten both you and her Ladyship. You're trying to get enormous damages. A huge sum of money . . .'

'Mr Rumpole, the amount of damages will be for me to decide.' The Judge was clearly in a talkative mood.

'Of course it will be. But,' I told Sir Mike, 'you have come to Court, and you stand there in that witness box, because you say you're outraged at the publication of one rather jolly photograph, when you allowed the whole of your private life to become fodder for the tabloid press. It doesn't make any sense at all, does it?'

And here I found again that I'd turned automatically to the Jury that wasn't there, as Dame Phillida reminded me. 'That Jury box is empty, Mr Rumpole. Perhaps an Old Bailey Jury wouldn't have noticed that you haven't dealt with the vital issue in this case – which is whether there was a breach of confidence. After signing the agreement to keep the press out, a photograph was taken. That has nothing to do with this gentleman's marriages, successful or not.' At this Sir Mike got another judicial smile, which he accepted with a slight bow, a fairly stiff inclination from his hips.

'Perhaps you'll deal with that issue in the morning, Mr Rumpole? Very well. Ten-thirty tomorrow.' Phillida clearly felt her day's work was done.

As we all made bows to the departing Judge, Liz Probert, who was with me as a Junior to lend a hand and take a note, assessed the situation. 'Do you think she fancies him?'

'I'm afraid so. There's no accounting for tastes.'

'You're giving each other a pretty bad time, you and Dame Philly.'

'That's because we're old friends.' By now the Judge had gone and we were gathering up our papers.

'Are you going to deal with the breach of confidence tomorrow?' Liz asked the question to which I had, as yet, no answer. 'I mean, wasn't there obviously a breach?'

'All right,' I conceded. 'What's the defence to that?'

Liz considered a moment and then suggested, 'Public interest?'

'Public interest we haven't got,' I had to admit. 'Public amusement, certainly. Public laughs, perhaps, but not public interest. No. We haven't got any of that.'

In saying which I was, as about so many things connected with my great privacy case, entirely wrong.

All the way home on the Underground I was repeating this magic phrase: 'the public interest'. It meant, no doubt, something the public needed to know, useful information. Did they need to know, for instance, that Mrs Justice Phillida Erskine-Brown was fatally attracted to over-confident, powerfully built, middle-aged men with unpleasant opinions on a wide range of subjects? Would the wheels of justice turn more smoothly if this information was widely disseminated? I was in a mood to think that it might be so. There might also be some value in the knowledge that Liz Probert, our Chambers' nearest approach to a young firebrand of the left, had joined her University Conservative Club. What, I wondered, could the public learn from the younger Claude Erskine-Brown's passionate love affair with a young actress in Grimsby? Nothing very much at all, I was forced to admit.

Such were the thoughts that were running through my head when I pushed open the door of our mansion flat and heard the television set booming. When I entered our sitting-room I found the screen filled with the head and shoulders of what looked like a gnome-like figure, with cropped hair and a beard which covered most of the lower half of his face with a sort of dusky shadow. He was saying something of no particular interest about political fundraising and across his chest ran the caption 'Lord Hindle, Party Treasurer and Fundraiser'. Hilda was engaged in writing a letter to one of her numerous school friends.

'Do turn him off, Rumpole.' She Who Must Be Obeyed had decided to use me as her remote control. 'He calls himself Lord Hindle, apparently a long-time friend of the Prime Minister, and he's a most deadly bore.'

'I don't believe in Party funding through taxation. That's not what the public wants. We have our supporters, giving anything from half a million to a few pounds, because they're people committed to us. They believe in our core values.' Lord Hindle had what's become known as an Estuary accent, a voice which has had all traces of personality filtered out of it, and he spoke slowly, deliberately, as though he was giving instructions to a roomful of dim-witted underlings who might not understand a word he said.

'Do turn him off, Rumpole. I'm trying to write to Dodo Mackintosh, and he's driving me mad!'

'I'm sorry.' I was standing very close to the television set. 'I need to look at him, I'll turn off the sound.' Deprived of his voice, his Lordship was only a face, but a face I was sure I'd seen somewhere before. I'd run through a long gallery of faces, many of villains, some of respectable citizens, before I suddenly remembered.

So I dusted off the old magnifying glass we kept in a drawer of the writing desk and carried out some further research. Then I dialled the home number Gervase Johnson had given me.

'Who on earth are you trying to telephone, Rumpole?' Hilda was watching me closely.

'Gervase Johnson. The journalist who wrote my profile for the *Fortress*.'

'They never used that profile, did they?'

'Hello. It's Rumpole.'

It was my lucky evening. Gervase Johnson was at home and sounded relatively sober. He was apologetic. 'I'm sorry they never used that profile of yours for the *Fortress*.'

'Perhaps they didn't think you were interesting enough,' Hilda called across the room.

'They didn't think you told me enough about your private life,' Gervase muttered in my ear.

'Never mind about my private life,' I spoke briskly. 'My private life's not the point at the moment. It's the private lives of other people. Are you at home? I'll come round and see you. I need your help desperately, old darling. I'm afraid it's going to take some time.'

It did, but I have to say that Gervase, once the situation was explained to him, joined me with enthusiasm. We travelled together to the *Fortress* offices in Canary Wharf, searched files, got help from the picture desk and ate bacon and eggs in the all-night canteen. I was lucky to have found in Gervase an old-fashioned journalist, one who was genuinely excited by the idea of discovering the truth.

The cold light of dawn breaking over the Gloucester Road found me shaving, and while I did so singing an old music-hall song much enjoyed by my father.

> 'They hadn't been married for a month or so
> When underneath her thumb went Jim.
> Isn't it a pity that the likes of her
> Should marry with the likes of him!'

'Do be quiet, Rumpole!' Hilda's cry of protest emerged from the bedroom and arrived through the bathroom's open door. 'What on earth are you singing for?'

'I'm singing,' I shouted back, 'because I think I might be in the public interest at last.'

'Mr Rumpole,' Phillida was still in her severe judicial mode, 'I hope you'll deal with the issue of breach of confidence today.'

'I certainly will,' I told her, and resisted the temptation to add, 'Why don't you just sit back and enjoy it?' By now Queen's Bench Court Four was beginning to feel more like home, someone had actually said good morning to me in the robing room, and the solid figure of Sir Mike was waiting for me in the witness box.

'Can you help me? Your holiday in St Lucia was a year ago last January?'

'That's right.'

'No doubt you went there to get a glimpse of the sun.'

Phillida smiled at the witness again.

'We didn't get much of it here. Yes, Mr Rumpole.'

'And in the following month your firm won the contract to supply a massive quantity of new beds to National Health Hospitals?'

'We did indeed. And production is going very well. In fact, I'm delighted to say we're ahead of schedule,' the witness reported to the Judge with pride.

'There were rumours going round that you got that contract because you gave a massive but unrecorded amount to Government funds.'

'There are always those sorts of rumours when there's a big contract.'

'We don't want evidence of mere rumours, Mr Rumpole.'

Phillida was still on the warpath. 'We want to deal with hard facts.'

'That is exactly what I mean to provide,' I said to reassure her and then turned back to the witness. 'It was suggested that you fixed the deal up with Lord Hindle. The Party treasurer and trusted political adviser to the Government.'

'There's not a word of truth in that suggestion.'

'Not a word of truth,' Phillida made a note.

'You went further than that, didn't you? You said you'd never even met Lord Hindle.'

'I may have said something like that.'

'You said exactly that, didn't you?'

For the first time the witness looked uncomfortable. He hesitated, looked for help to Hugo Winterton who was staring, with great interest, at the ceiling, and protested, 'I can't be expected to remember everything I said a year ago.'

'Then let me help you. Do you remember giving an interview to Gervase Johnson for a profile in the *Daily Fortress*?'

'Yes, I remember that.'

'Then perhaps you'll listen to what you said.' I had Gervase's unreliable instrument in my hand, its red light glowing. In it was the tape he had found of the Smedley interview. I pressed a button. The machine was silent.

'Shake it!' whispered Gervase, who was now sitting behind me. I tried. Still silence.

'Hit it then. Not too hard.'

I gave the antique device a brisk slap and it spoke out at last to the Court. We heard Gervase's question. 'It's been suggested you did a deal with Lord Hindle and made a big contribution to the Party?' And Sir Mike's clear answer, 'I've never met Lord Hindle or spoken to him. I had no connection with him whatever before the contract.'

'That's your voice, isn't it?' was my next question.

'It seems to be.'

'And it's your voice telling a thumping lie?'

'Of course it's not a lie.'

'Is that your answer?'

'I've already told you –'

'Very well. Let's come if we can to the night of the party at the Sugar and Spice Bar.'

'It was a private party.'

'Exactly. For your friends?'

'For people I'd invited, yes.'

'Just take another look at the photograph, will you? I take it that was your table – you're dancing near it with your headdress and there's an empty seat.'

'That was my table, yes.'

'Just have a look at the other people at your table.'

'It's difficult to see in the shadows.'

'Just try. It's not too difficult, is it? Can you make out a small man at the table. A man with close-cut hair and the dark shadow of a beard?'

'You mean next to the tall blonde lady, Mr Rumpole?' Phillida had got her magnifying glass out and was studying the photograph with interest.

'That's the one. Your Ladyship has it!' I congratulated her.

'I'm not sure who that is.' Sir Mike was playing for time.

'Then let me help you.' We hadn't wasted our time in the picture department of the *Fortress*. Thanks to Gervase, they had blown up the picture of Gerry Hindle and another man watching Sir Michael's dance of joy with the bra.

'That's the man you said you'd never even met, isn't it?'

Now the witness was looking hopefully from one enlarged picture to the other. All he could say was 'It's like him, I agree.'

'It *is* him. I'm afraid you've got to agree. So now we know

133

what this case is all about. You don't care who sees you dancing about festooned with underwear, but you didn't want anyone to see that you're a liar who met the Party Treasurer and no doubt paid your money and took your contract. That's what we're all here for, isn't it? We're going through this legal farce to protect another bit of political sleaze. Isn't that the truth of the matter?'

'Mr Rumpole.' It was Dame Phillida who answered, but a changed, distressed and deeply serious Dame Phillida, who looked at the witness and now turned away from him as though she could no longer stand the sight. 'Mr Rumpole, I take it you are alleging that it's in the public's interest that this photograph should be published to disclose what may have been an improper agreement about a government contract?' She said that and we were friends again.

'Your Ladyship puts it much more clearly than I could.' I gave her what I hope was a charming smile.

'And I take it you're asking for an adjournment so you can amend your pleadings to cover these new allegations.'

'Your Ladyship is right,' I told her. 'That's exactly what I'm asking for.'

The adjournment turned out to be very short. We waited outside Queen's Bench Court Four while further down the corridor Sir Mike snarled at his legal team as though, if his case really had taken a turn for the worse, it was entirely their fault. Meanwhile, the irrepressible Rankin was saying 'Excellent!' and 'What japes!' at regular intervals and Liz Probert was trying to draft a new defence. Then Hugo's Junior came like a herald to suggest I meet his leader at a neutral point halfway down the corridor, between our opposing armies.

'I think I've talked a bit of sense into him.' My learned friend offered me a small cigar, which I accepted gratefully.

'It's no good our going on with this. You'll only get him further and further up shit creek. I'm going to tell the Judge that, out of respect to an old established family newspaper, we're calling the whole thing off, and of course we'll have to pay your costs.'

'That suits me very well,' I told him. 'You tell Dame Phillida that. She'll be sorry to see him go.'

'Not so sorry, I think, after his performance this morning,' my opponent had to admit. 'I expect you'll be glad to return to the Old Bailey, won't you?'

'Away from this almighty sleaze,' I agreed. 'It'll be nice to get back to a bit of ordinary decent crime.'

We had dropped a small stone into the muddy waters of politics and the ripples spread. Much to everyone's surprise and regret it was discovered that Sir Mike's contribution to Party funds hadn't been recorded or disclosed. This may have been due to a computer breakdown or some similar act of God, the relevant minister told Parliament. Sir Mike's generosity had nothing whatever to do with the contract for hospital beds, Slumberwell being quite clearly the only firm to offer competitive prices and a dependable delivery date. Lord Hindle had been staying with friends in St Lucia and they had taken him to the party in the Sugar and Spice Bar, a fact which Sir Mike may have quite understandably forgotten. The Standards Committee was considering the matter, and had it well in hand. When the Opposition asked questions, the answers were reassuring. There would be the fullest and fairest investigation and a full report would be made to the House as soon as possible. Meanwhile, the Government was delighted to announce that the target for the provision of new hospital beds would certainly be reached by 1st October, although, of course, the Government couldn't absolutely guarantee this date, which was only, in fact, a 'desirable' target. At the moment there were more serious matters to discuss, such as the recycling of outdated mobile telephones.

It was during these great national events that Claude Erskine-Brown entered my room, slumped into my client's chair and spoke in a voice of doom.

'Sometimes,' he complained, 'I can't understand Philly.'

'The learned Judge,' I had to admit, 'is subject to sudden mood swings. What's happened now?'

'She's absolutely furious about Mercy Grandison's book. It's come out, you know, and she sent her clerk out to buy a copy. She said she wanted to read about my great passion.'

'And now she's cross about what Mercy wrote?'

'No. She's cross about what Mercy didn't write.'

'Well, go on. Tell me. What didn't Mercy write?'

'She wrote nothing about me, Rumpole.'

'Nothing, Claude?'

'Absolutely nothing. She dealt with her days in the Grimsby Rep. in considerable detail. But there was no mention of my name, even. And certainly not of the great experience which has remained with me all my life.'

'It's possible, isn't it, she was just being discreet?'

'You haven't read *The Wandering Star*, Rumpole. There's absolutely nothing discreet about it. No. Philly thinks she left it out because it wasn't of the slightest importance to her.'

'Your wife takes a harsh view?'

'Merciless. "This great affair you're so proud of, Claude," she said. "You see your old girlfriend's simply forgotten all about it."'

'You should never have told her, Claude,' was all I could find to say.

'I know, Rumpole. I jumped before I came to the stile.'

'An unwise thing to do. Don't worry, it'll pass. Dame

Phillida can make mistakes with the best of us. She had a momentary affection for a crooked bed-maker, but it's all over now. She'll forget Mercy.'

'Just like Mercy's forgotten me.' Erskine-Brown's tone was bitter.

'It's the private life, Claude. Just let it rest in peace. It's a great mistake to try to protect it. It always leads to trouble.'

Rumpole and the Vanishing Juror

The proudest of our national treasures, to rank with Wordsworth, the plays of Shakespeare and the great British breakfast
– that is to say the Jury – is not, of course, a single twelve-
headed monster, swinging from one side to the other until it
arrives, with ponderous deliberation, at its single-minded
decision. It's a random collection of disparate individuals, and
may include a *Telegraph*-reading accountant, a well-meaning
sociology teacher who started the day with organic muesli
and the *Guardian*, a jobbing builder who would like to see the
Black Cap put on at the end of murder trials, a Sikh minicab
driver, a trouser-suited businesswoman with the *Financial
Times*, a hair stylist from a unisex hairdressing salon whose
jeans seem in constant danger of sliding off her narrow hips,
and a worried grandmother. Often these apparently predict-
able types can spring surprising verdicts. The muesli-eating
teacher may believe that prison works, and the builder may
be a stickler for the presumption of innocence.

Their verdicts may be unpredictable, but the experienced
Old Bailey hack can usually identify his friends and spot his
enemies. The friendly juror often smiles at him first thing in
the morning, smiles, at least, at his jokes, and even shows
signs of impatience when the hack's flow is interrupted by an
unsympathetic Judge. The hostile juror will cross his or her
arms and stare at the ceiling during your most persuasive

speeches, and raise his or her eyebrows and sigh heavily during your client's story that what might have looked like house-breaking implements were merely in his car for repairs to the shed in his allotment, and laugh sycophantically at the Judge's poor attempts at comedy.

The difficult decision is whether to encourage your friends, to favour them with the first meaningful look when you score a palpable hit in cross-examination and so strengthen their sinews and summon up their blood for a fearless acquittal; or should you devote all your energies to converting your enemies? You can flatter them with the meaningful looks and intimate smiles and hope against hope that they haven't decided you're an insincere and money-grabbing protector of the criminals who ought, if there was any real justice in the world, to be *in* the dock beside the undoubtedly guilty customer.

In the case of *R.* v. *Skeate*, another murder which I managed to do alone and without a leader, the crime was so savagely pointless, the victim so beautiful, that hostility to the admittedly unattractive man in the dock blew like an icy wind from the Jury box, and friendly faces were as hard to find as contraceptives in the Vatican. There was, however, one exception to the general line-up of pursed lips and folded arms. Number four juror sat listening to me with a smile that shone like a good deed in a naughty world.

The name she answered to, when the Clerk of the Court read out the list of jurors, was Kathleen Brewster. She was a woman probably in her fifties, who always arrived a little late, as though she had overslept, or had to get a small grandchild ready for school, or been involved in the usual immobility of the Circle Line, or left her glasses somewhere and turned up, in a moment of confusion, in the wrong Court. She would push her way, murmuring apologies, past the knees of frozen-faced jurors and then flash the friendliest smile, one that not only wished me well but promised me her full attention.

So as you can imagine, I concentrated on stoking the fires of Kathleen Brewster's admiration in the hope that she would warm the cold hearts of fellow members of the Jury. All was going well until, one morning in the middle of the trial, as rare things will she vanished.

The events that led to the untimely disappearance of Kathleen Brewster had begun many months before on Hampstead Heath. Two middle-aged men were jogging together early on a Sunday morning, accompanied by their long-haired terrier, Gloria. She was seen to leave the two friends and disappear, yapping excitedly, into a patch of scrub near to what's called, inappropriately in this particular instance, the Vale of Health. When they tried to extricate their dog from the bushes, the two friends uncovered a long, slim leg, dressed in jeans and trainers. Further investigation revealed, to their horror, the body of a slim, dark-skinned woman, perhaps in her early thirties, her undoubted beauty disfigured by what was later described as manual strangulation. Her neck was badly bruised and her face bloated. The police investigation started with a stroke of luck: one jeans pocket was found to contain some loose change, a crumpled ten-pound note, a driving licence in the name of Pamela McDonnell, and an address in West Heath Road.

When they went to the address, the police found an eight-year-old boy being looked after by two of Pamela's girlfriends, who were waiting, with increasing anxiety, for the return of his mother . . . She never came back, but pictures of her, unwounded and unblemished, a sparkling Jamaican beauty, began to appear in all the papers and, not unexpectedly, the nation took her to its heart.

Pamela was born in Kilburn, the child of immigrant parents. Her mother cleaned hospitals, her father worked on the buses. She went to school regularly and sang in the church choir. After her son Cameron was born, she worked for all sorts of charitable organizations. She also had theatrical ambitions and had given her Helen of Troy in *Doctor Faustus* in a venue over a pub in Kilburn.

It then emerged that to add to her income, and to pay for extra lessons for Cameron, she worked on three evenings a week as a lap dancer in the Candy Crocodile restaurant in a narrow street behind Leicester Square, which provided such entertainment for its customers. Her work in this department of show business did nothing to detract from her posthumous popularity. Her beauty, her hard work for her son, even her athletic dancing in a venue where the customers were strictly ordered to look but not to touch, won her nothing but sympathy, and her cruel and inexplicable death cried out for revenge. The *Daily Post* offered fifty thousand pounds for information leading to the conviction of her murderer and the police were under constant pressure to find a likely suspect. It came as a relief to everyone when, before very long, such a suspect was found. The public breathed a sigh of relief and looked forward eagerly to the trial at the Old Bailey. As the *Daily Post* headline put it, 'Let Justice be done for Pamela at last'.

The man arrested was billed as Neville J. Skeate, aged thirty-two, unmarried, a clerk, living in Streatham. He appeared briefly in a South London Magistrates Court, where he was described as wearing a dark business suit, a white shirt and a tie. He answered to his name in a loud, clear voice and was remanded for the police to make further enquiries. What was significant, from the point of view of the Rumpole career since my resurrection, was the fact that the solicitor on duty at the local Court was none other than my old friend and provider of life-giving briefs, Bonny Bernard. I got an early insight into the police enquiries and the case against the man who had made only a fleeting appearance in the Magistrates Court. The facts, if true, were enough to chill the blood, even that of an Old Bailey hack well used to the horror and violence which bubble too near the surface of our so-called civilized society.

Neville Skeate was more than just a clerk. He was, he was proud to proclaim, the founder and leading light of the Ninth Day Elamites, a small and completely ineffective group of what appeared, to an old barrister dedicated to the vital importance of reasonable doubt, to be religious nut cases. The cause they had adopted was that of purging the Greater London area, including the adjacent suburbs, of sin, corruption, perverse and lustful behaviour and the 'worship of false Gods'. They took their title from the people of Elam who, led by their king, made war upon the people of Sodom and Gomorrah, the sinful cities of the plain whose punishment and destruction is described in the book of Genesis. So Skeate was by day a harmless and useful clerk in the Public Records Office; but by night he sallied forth to denounce gay bars in Soho, strip clubs, massage parlours and such centres of the esoteric art of lap dancing as the Candy Crocodile off Leicester Square. He would hand out leaflets filled with dreadful warnings about the dire fate of citizens of Sodom, with which town London was now undoubtedly twinned. He and his adherents would shout abuse and biblical texts at the patrons or the performers as they came out of such places. The reaction of most of the citizens greeted with such alarming threats was to hurry past with an embarrassed smile in search of the last train back to Beckenham or Crouch End and so out of the brimstone area. Unlike most of my clients, Neville Skeate made no effort to conceal his identity. All his pamphlets bore his name as 'Chief Witness of the Ninth Day Elamites'. He signed letters to the various night haunts he visited and to the local newspapers, which hardly ever printed them.

The Candy Crocodile was, it seemed, a sink of iniquity which attracted Neville Skeate's particular attention. He would wait outside it until, almost at dawn, the last customers and then the girls emerged to climb into their waiting minicabs and be driven home to bed. He denounced them all, but shouted loudest at Pamela, easily distinguishable as the only Jamaican girl in the group. What he said seemed ridiculous when I came to read it in print, but called out in an empty street by a pale-faced man filled with hatred it must have sounded alarming. 'Look at her!' he would call out. 'The Slime Pit! . . . The Strumpet! . . . The Daughter of Adultery. . . . The Whore of Babylon!' And, after other such terms of endearment, he threatened, according to the girls who worked with Pamela, to strike her with blindness, and condemned her to fire, brimstone and an early death.

Not all of these threats were intelligible to the girls from the Candy Crocodile, who had, at best, only a sketchy knowledge of the book of Genesis. Some of them reacted with fury and outrage, and looked, always in vain, for a wandering policeman. The bouncer from the club sometimes came out and chased Neville away, and once caught him and beat him up, causing bruises which Neville wore with the pride of a wounded soldier when he resumed, and even increased, his attacks. Pamela, according to her friends and fellow workers, laughed at him, and took his threats of her death and destruction as a joke. The case for the prosecution was that they were made, in fact, in deadly earnest.

*

'Rumpole!' Hilda said this in the brisk, call-to-order voice which I knew from experience would not be the prelude to good news. 'I've been talking to Doctor McClintock about you. I was right.'

'Oh yes?' I tried to say it in a casual manner, as though it were an event of the smallest significance. 'Pleased, was he, that I'm back again in full working order?'

'I'm not sure you *are* in full working order, Rumpole. Not sure at all. That's why I had a word with Doctor McClintock.'

'And he reassured you, did he?'

'No. He didn't reassure me. He said he hadn't seen you for some time. Not this year, he said. Can that be true?'

'Possibly.' At my age you steer clear of the quack in case he tells you you've got something you didn't want to know about. Of course, I didn't tell She Who Must Be Obeyed that. She is the fearless sort, who positively enjoys check-ups. 'There's been a considerable pressure of work lately. I may have this rather sensational murder case.'

'Don't worry about murders for the moment, Rumpole. You should concentrate on keeping yourself alive. Doctor McClintock asked me if you seemed to be short of breath after taking exercise.'

'Well, you know the answer to that. I never take exercise.'

'Exactly! Peter McClintock was deeply shocked. He wouldn't believe it at first. But I swore it was true.'

'And you were right, Hilda. Absolutely right.'

'Peter insists that you should take some sort of exercise.'

'Quite right! I'll remember that. I do take a brisk stroll round to the tobacconist in Fleet Street to buy my small cigars.'

'Don't talk rubbish, Rumpole! What the Doctor recommends in your case is some light bicycling.'

'Oh, I'm afraid that's impossible.'

'Don't be ridiculous! Of course it's not impossible.'

'I'm afraid it is. To go bicycling nowadays you have to wear a hat shaped like a peanut. That's enforced by law, I believe. And rubber shorts. Black with a sort of white line down them. I mean I couldn't possibly turn up in Chambers dressed like that. Besides which I might be run into by a bus and asphyxiated by petrol fumes. I gave up bicycling long before I did the Penge Bungalow Murders.'

'You're not going to bicycle out on the street, Rumpole. I wouldn't dream of suggesting that.'

'Where do you want me to do it, then? On some sort of bicycle racetrack?'

'Of course not. You will be on a stationary bicycle. It won't be going anywhere.'

'What on earth's the point of that, then? Has his anxiety about my health caused the good Doctor McClintock to lose his marbles?'

'The point of it, Rumpole, is to help you to train yourself up, to lose some of that unnecessary weight. To open up your tubes and help your breathing. To make you sweat a little and get to know your own body. I've taken up joint married membership at the Lysander Health Club in Iverna Gardens. They do special terms for married couples. Two for the price of one. They've got exercise bikes, of course, as well as all the other equipment.'

'All the other equipment' sounded, I thought, extremely sinister.

'I'm afraid I've got to go,' I told Hilda as I made for the door. 'A conference in Brixton.'

At that moment prison sounded a far more attractive proposition than the Lysander Health Club.

'If they could find ten Just Men in Sodom and Gomorrah, Mr Rumpole, the Lord promised not to send down fire.

They couldn't be found, Mr Rumpole. So the cities of the plain were destroyed by fire and brimstone. You remember that?'

'Not personally. I may be getting on a bit, but –'

'They looked, but ten Just Men couldn't be found.'

'Are you saying that there are less than ten Just Men in Greater London? Please don't tell the Jury that. There'll be twelve of them and I'm sure they'll like to think of themselves as Just Men. And Women, of course.'

Neville Skeate looked at me as though he couldn't understand a word I was saying. He was tall, colourless, with a pale face, glasses, and large, bony hands kept folded on his lap. He looked what he was, a minor clerk in a government department, someone no one noticed or paid much attention to. He went home, I suspected, to a lonely bedsit, a meal to reheat bought from the supermarket on the way home. A man with few relatives, and a friend or two from the office, he was apparently nondescript and inoffensive. And yet when he spoke, a disturbingly rich and deep voice came out of him – a voice capable of issuing commands to the few dotty adherents of the Ninth Day Elamites. It was a voice, and this was the most alarming thing about him, of passionate conviction.

'I shall tell the Jury that the slime pits of this city shall be destroyed utterly and sinners shall taste death.'

'If that's what you're going to say,' I looked at him with as much detachment as I could manage, 'I'd better keep you out of the witness box.'

Bonny Bernard had brought me the Ninth Day Elamite like a birthday present which I would unwrap with eager anticipation. He thought I would be overjoyed by a brief in a sensational murder which was bound to hit the headlines.

'Legal Aid said we could either have a QC or a Senior

Junior,' Bernard told me. 'I said we would settle for you as the Senior Junior, Mr Rumpole. Well, it'll save them a bit of money and I was sure you'd jump at the offer.'

'That was good of you. Extremely good.' I had read the papers and wasn't sure that I ought not to be more wary of Bonny bearing gifts.

'I knew you'd be grateful. A case like this, I told your clerk Henry, will bring the snap back into Mr Rumpole's celery. It'll do him more good than all the tonics and treatments in the world.'

Would it? Perhaps I *was* getting past it, but I couldn't open the papers in *Skeate* without a feeling of almost unbearable sadness at the senselessness of the murdered beauty, the loneliness of the waiting child and the terrible obsession of the clerk whose mind had been turned to hatred disguised as religion. Civilization may not have come all that far, I thought, but at least we no longer use fire and brimstone as the answer to unconventional sex or tasteless entertainment. My first thought had been a plea of insanity, or at least diminished responsibility, but the doctors could find no recognized mental illness. No doubt Neville Skeate had an unfortunate tendency to take the Scriptures too literally, they said, but this was a view shared by creationists all over the world, and they couldn't all be certified insane.

The most encouraging way of approaching Neville Skeate's case was to consider the prosecution evidence. There were plenty of witnesses to the death threats directed particularly at Pamela outside the Candy Crocodile, but none of the act itself. He had been identified as having been often seen on Hampstead Heath, where it seems he went not to run for exercise but to denounce, whenever he could, the male homosexuals who met, and occasionally made love, in certain remote and wooded areas. He agreed that he had once or twice seen Pamela jogging, but denied he had ever accosted or threatened her on the heath. When the trainers and tracksuit trousers he wore on such rural visits were inspected, minute particles of sandy soil similar to that where Pamela was found were discovered clinging to the soles and sides of his shoes. So the case against Neville Skeate seemed to come down to his threats specifically directed at the dead woman and his possible presence at the scene of the crime.

'You called her the Whore of Babylon?' I asked him when we met in Brixton Prison.

'On many occasions, when I was outside the house of slime pits.'

'You promised her an early death?'

'I did. And my promise was fulfilled.'

'Because you killed her?'

Did I have a hope, contrary to all my principles as a defending hack, that he would admit it and have to plead guilty and we would soon be rid of him? But, for better or for worse, we remained in business as he said, 'No, Mr Rumpole. I never killed her.'

'Would you be prepared to say you greatly regret her death?' I'd hoped for some reasonable words he might repeat to the Jury; but I hoped in vain.

'Do I regret the death of weeds that are thrown on the bonfire? No, I don't regret her death, Mr Rumpole. In fact, I rejoice in it.'

'You think she deserved to die because she went, what do they call it, lap dancing?'

'She behaved as I named her. The Whore of Babylon.'

'How do you know? I've never seen anyone lap dancing. Have you?'

'Of course I haven't.'

'So you would have condemned her to death for something

you know absolutely nothing about. Is that what you're really saying?'

'I know very well what she did. She revelled in it. That's what I know. She revelled in the sins of the city.'

'So she had to die?'

'Not my decision, Mr Rumpole. The decision of one greater than I.'

'What the prosecution are saying is that you might have taken her life in your hands and strangled Pamela.'

'I might have, Mr Rumpole. I might have done anything. But those above me had other plans for her. That is all I have to say.'

I looked at my client. What on earth was I to do about him? I had never, in all the long years I had spent round the criminal Courts, come across a customer for whom I felt more good, old-fashioned, honest loathing. So the answer to my question was, of course, that I must defend him to the very best of my ability.

There seemed to me to have been a time, in my boyhood, when bicycling was a source of pleasure. Not struggling up a hill, of course, not pedalling through rain with frozen fingers on a slithery road, but coasting down a gradual incline on a spring morning with a light breeze behind you and the three-speed Raleigh ticking happily. This was an experience to be ranked with the first gulp of Château Thames Embankment after a satisfactory verdict for a grateful client. But bicycling in the Lysander Club was a different story. There was no fresh breeze, no bright green leaves of spring, merely air conditioning, a pervading smell of massage oil and piped Caribbean music. What was worse was that after the most prolonged and industrious pedalling you found yourself going nowhere at all. It was a most frustrating experience, only to be compared to conducting a trial in an empty courtroom, with no Judge, no Jury, and absolutely no end in view.

There was a little clock on the handlebars of the bike, which I was instructed to keep flickering above a certain mark. It was, I'm afraid, dropping like my spirits, as my journey began to feel like a long path uphill to infinity, when a voice behind me called, 'Well done, Rumpole! We'll have you in the Tour de France yet.'

I turned to see Luci with an 'i', wearing thick leggings as though equipped for a hike through Outer Mongolia.

'Luci! You're not a fellow sufferer at the Lysander Club?' It was a Saturday morning, and an odd way, I thought, for anyone, including me, to spend their day off work.

'Yeah! Yeah! Yeah!' She had taken to repeating these three affirmations rapidly, like machine-gun fire. 'I persuaded Hilda to join at the last Chambers party. We have such fun here together, whenever I can get time off.'

'Fun?' I was, I must confess, puzzled. 'You have fun with Hilda?'

'Of course. Don't you?'

'In a manner of speaking. She went off shopping. She said she'd feed me on nothing but organically grown rocket salad and vegetarian rissoles unless I promised to spend at least an hour in the gym. I suppose you might call that "fun".'

'It's because she loves you, Rumpole. She wants you to keep fit, now that it seems you're not going to die. Come on, I'll buy you a coffee.'

I had dismounted, perhaps in the hope of some such invitation. The bike didn't need parking, or pushing round to the sheds, and I left it standing, ready for the next traveller with nowhere to go.

I sat with Luci in a small bar where people in white dressing-gowns were whispering into their mobile phones and reading newspapers. I was trying to grapple with a new thought Luci had put in my mind. I had assumed (was it too rashly?) that Hilda wanted to send me bicycling because that would prevent me slinking off to Pommeroy's under the pretence of having to pick up a brief in Chambers, or as an exercise in the power of her will to unfix my determination. Had I, for too long, totally misunderstood She Who Must Be Obeyed? I drank coffee that was so weak it needed a long go on the bicycle machine, and changed the subject. 'All going well in the Marketing of Chambers, is it?' It had to be one of the dullest questions I had ever asked.

'All right. Henry still looks at me as though I was in there to pinch the cheques and insult the solicitors. Sam Ballard's as charming as always . . .'

I thought about that. Could someone who found Soapy Sam charming be trusted in her interpretation of Hilda's motives?

'Erskine-Brown's started to hug me for longer than it takes to show corporate solidarity and wants to take me out to lunch. Oh, hello, Dermot. You're looking good!'

The man she addressed as Dermot had a red face, against which his hair and moustache seemed as white as the driven snow. He was wearing scarlet shorts and a T-shirt which said, 'My wife went to Eilat and all she bought me was this lousy T-shirt'. I couldn't tell from a casual glance whether he was as good as Luci thought. He may have been a fraudster with an engaging appearance.

'Hilda's not here.' Dermot stated an obvious fact.

'Not today,' Luci told him. 'This is Hilda's husband. Rumpole, this is Dermot. He does the sport on Thamesway Radio.'

'Pity, that!' He gave me a quick smile, a flash of pure white dentures. 'We have a lot of fun when Hilda's around, don't we, Luci?'

'A few laughs, yes.'

'A few laughs?' I was longing for further particulars, but Dermot, looking at me as though my grey flannels and striped shirt were in some way humorous, said, 'Oh, you're the legal beagle, aren't you? The chap who defends all those crooks.'

'He's defending that man for the murder on Hampstead Heath,' Luci told him.

'That lovely girl!' Dermot looked at me with stern disapproval. 'And that creepy little bastard strangled her!'

'I'm not sure doing that case does much good for the image of Chambers.' Luci was equally disapproving.

'Of course it does. It shows the world that even creepy little bastards need defending, just as much as beautiful girls, sports commentators or anyone else. And the creepier they are, the more they need help. They're innocent until they're proved guilty.' I had said it all before, but I'd go on saying it to anyone who didn't understand.

'I suppose you think you'll get him off.' Dermot the sports commentator sounded contemptuous.

'I may do,' I told him. But the day before, we had been served an additional statement which made creepy Neville's chances of walking free considerably less likely.

In a bizarre world of fire and brimstone, cities fallen into sin, a beautiful woman condemned to an arbitrary death, a child left motherless and a lonely clerk acting in what he conceived to be the service of a vengeful God, Court Number One at the Old Bailey seemed, on the morning the trial began, an oasis of sanity. It was presided over by Mr Justice Sloper, known as Beetle because of the strong lenses which gave his eyes a bulging and insect-like appearance. He did his best not to interrupt and was reasonably civil to barristers. I remember him as a prosecution Junior in the Penge Bungalow Murders, when we used to buy each other a Guinness during the lunch-time adjournment, much to the annoyance of our clients who thought, quite wrongly, that we were doing a deal behind their backs.

Now the prosecution was in the hands of Adrian Hoddinot, a tall and languid learned friend, who always said he merely stayed at the Bar for the sake of keeping his Great Dane, Ophelia, in the comfortable state to which she had become accustomed. He was high on my list of decent prosecutors and had, in fact, been a considerable help to me in the case of the Teenage Werewolf. The Jury looked seriously impressed by the horror and seriousness of the case they had read about in the papers; but I had no reason to think they wouldn't listen to anything the defence might have to offer. All this is only to say that the trial of Neville Skeate was about to be conducted by a reasonable body of men and women, the only representative of the fire-and-brimstone attitude to justice being the quiet clerk sitting in the dock with his great hands neatly folded.

The Court clerk read out the names of the jurors and they answered to them briskly. My future friend and ally was Number Four in the Jury box, sitting between a grey-haired man with a slight limp, who might have been a retired school-master, and a fidgety young man in an unstructured suit, perhaps a dealer in options and futures, who was no doubt counting the money he was missing in the City and wishing he was elsewhere. Number Four was asked if her name was Kathleen Brewster, to which she answered with a smiling 'Yes' as though it were her pleasure and privilege to be there. With the Jury roll-call over, she settled down to listen to Adrian Hoddinot as he opened the case for the prosecution.

After describing the finding of the body, and telling the Jury about the murdered girl, the prosecutor started to deal

with the case against my client. 'The defendant Skeate . . .'
No doubt determined to be fair, the dog-loving Adrian still
couldn't keep a note of anger and contempt out of his voice,
'adopted the habit of shouting abuse in such places as gay
bars and massage parlours . . .'

At this point I thought it right to rise and offer an objection.
'My Lord,' I said, 'may I, in all humility –' (a meaningless
phrase, inserted merely to give me time to decide how to
frame my objection. I didn't feel in the least humble that
morning), 'may I submit that this case has nothing whatever
to do with gay bars and massage parlours. A person may
object to many institutions, in my case it might be banks and
fast-food outlets, but such strong feelings might well fall far
short of the tendency to murder.'

I saw Kathleen Brewster stifle a giggle with the back of her
hand. Beetle Sloper glanced at her from the Bench and
seemed impressed with the success of my objection with a
front-row juror. 'Yes, Mr Hoddinot, I think Mr Rumpole has
a point there. Perhaps you should confine your evidence to
the place of entertainment where it is suggested that death
threats were uttered against Pamela McDonnell. The Candy
Caterpillar.'

'Crocodile, my Lord.'

'What did you say?'

'It's called the Candy Crocodile.'

'Yes, of course it is.' The Beetle seemed only mildly irritated
in an exchange typical of the vague misunderstandings which
haunt all criminal trials. What was more unusual was what I
noticed in other parts of the Court. Recovered from her giggle,
Kathleen was looking up at the public gallery, which was well
filled, as were the press benches. The character who seemed
to have attracted her attention was a fair-haired man, perhaps
in his thirties, wearing a dark suit but with a tan which looked

as though he might have lived in a climate sunnier than that of London, the city of sin. He was sitting in the first row of the public gallery. Listening carefully and taking notes, he seemed to have some deep interest in the trial.

'Did you hear my client call Pamela McDonnell a Slime Pit?'

'Something like that, yes.'

'And the Whore of Babylon?'

'I believe Babylon did come into it.'

'Was there a good deal about smiting the cities of sin?'

'He was threatening her. There were a lot of words. I didn't pay all that much attention to them.'

I was cross-examining the doorman and bouncer of the Candy Crocodile. Number Four juror, Kathleen Brewster, was watching my performance with approval.

'Perhaps you could help us about this, Mr Henry Parkin.' I gave the bouncer his full name. 'Wasn't a great deal of what he was saying quoted from the Old Testament of the Bible?'

'I wouldn't know about that. It sounded like threats to me.'

'A great deal of the Old Testament does consist of threats, does it not, Mr Rumpole?' The Beetle on the Bench was doing his best to follow the evidence.

'In a historical context, my Lord. There may be some mention of smiting and destroying with fire and brimstone, but I don't believe anyone feels threatened when they hear it read out in church on Sundays.'

My fan in the Jury box gave me a small chuckle, although most of her fellow jurors remained stony-faced.

'What I'm suggesting is that Neville Skeate was denouncing London as a wicked city, in a general sort of way.'

'He has told us,' the Beetle Judge was determined, unfortunately for my client, to see that the whole of the bouncer's evidence was remembered, 'that he heard your client threatening to kill Pamela McDonnell.'

'That's right. That's when I punched him.' My fan was no longer smiling and most of her fellow jurors looked as though they approved strongly of the bouncer's reaction to the Ninth Day Elamite's sermon.

'Are you sure you heard him threaten to kill her?' I was trying to make the best of a bad job.

'I heard that. Yes.'

'Haven't you ever heard these words used by people who mean nothing of the sort?'

'What're you saying, exactly?' Mr Parkin was puzzled.

'A mother angry with her child may say, "I'll kill you if you don't sit still on the bus." Or someone at work, "I'll kill that plumber if he doesn't turn up this afternoon."'

I looked at the Jury box. Number Four seemed to be trying hard to find this part of my cross-examination convincing, but she was the only one. Mr Parkin the bouncer was more helpful.

'I suppose I've heard something like that. At times.'

'And let's be quite clear about this. You never saw him attack her, or even touch her in any way?'

'He never touched her so far as I could see. No.'

'Thank you, Mr Parkin.'

I sat down. What more could I do? The dog-loving Adrian Hoddinot got up for a cunning re-examination.

'Mr Parkin, Mr Rumpole has suggested that some people might use the words "I'll kill you" without them necessarily meaning much at all.'

'I heard that, yes.'

'Is the difference between the child on the bus and the plumber and Pamela McDonnell that she actually ended up dead?'

Of course, I objected. Of course, the Judge disapproved. But the prosecutor had made an obvious point. Well, you can't possibly win them all down the Old Bailey, but Number Four in the Jury box looked sadly disappointed.

Through all this, Neville Skeate sat in the dock motionless, his great crude hands folded in his lap, his face only betraying the satisfied smile of those who feel sure they have God on their side.

I had an easier task with the soil expert found by the forensic science department of the Metropolitan Police to report on the specks of dirt found on the soles of Neville Skeate's trainers.

'There were no footprints that matched his shoes found near the body?'

'It had rained in the night. I understand there were no clear footprints.' The forensic witness was young and considerably overweight. He had a thin, reedy voice and the bright, enquiring eyes of someone who spends their time examining minute particles of dirt in the hope of finding some evidence of guilt.

'You say there was some soil and grass on Skeate's shoes?'

'He had been standing on grass, yes.'

'A fascinating discovery!' I congratulated him. 'So he might have been standing on any lawn or bit of grassland in England? Not much of a help in this enquiry, is it?'

'No. But the soil. It was acidic clay, basically.'

'Ah yes, of course. The soil. Can you tell us how many spots in Greater London or the Home Counties might have similar patches of acidic clay soil?'

'Not all that many, perhaps, with exactly the same pH acidity figure of 5.5. Not in precisely those proportions.'

'Not all that many. But some?'

'Perhaps some.'

'So it's possible that Neville Skeate had been standing on some of these other patches of sandy soil, and was nowhere near Hampstead Heath when Pamela McDonnell met her untimely death? Can we rule that out?'

'I suppose,' the young master of the speck of dirt had to admit, 'we can't rule that out entirely.'

'Bricks without straw,' I had to tell Bonny Bernard when we emerged for lunchtime adjournment from Court Number One.

'Perhaps.' My favourite instructing solicitor wasn't always encouraging. 'But you do make them particularly well.'

We were trying to console ourselves with slices of cold pie and pints of Guinness in the pub opposite the Old Bailey, when a voice behind me was heard to say, 'It's an education to watch you in action, Mr Rumpole.'

I turned to see a sun-tanned face and a helmet of fairish hair, and to meet the white-toothed smile of a boyish man in a dark, fashionably tailored suit.

'As a very junior member of the legal profession, it would be an honour to buy you two hard-working gentlemen lunch.'

After I had made a vague and happily unsuccessful protest, and after he had ordered himself a drink and handed a couple of notes to the barman, I asked him where he practised law.

'Abroad, mainly. Middle East. Arab Emirates. All commercial work. I'm afraid you'd find it very dull. I just happened to be in England and I read you were defending a murderer.'

'He's not a murderer yet. Not till he's found guilty.'

'Still, it's only a matter of time.' He seemed to take it for granted.

It was then that I remembered where I'd seen him. Of course, he was the man in the public gallery who my favourite juror had stared at for a long moment on the first day of the trial.

'You've been listening to all the evidence?'

'Oh, I couldn't miss a moment.' He seemed so anxious to talk that I couldn't finish a sentence. 'I'm so admiring the way you're making a hopeless case sound as though it actually had a run.'

I hadn't minded when Bonny Bernard said it, but I resented this instant presumption of guilt from a complete stranger. 'I don't think you'll know whether or not there's anything in it until the Jury comes back,' I told him. 'You may see some surprises yet.'

'I shouldn't have said that, I suppose.' His smile was now faintly apologetic. 'But you must know yourself, Mr Rumpole, with all your great experience of the law, that poor old religious maniac hasn't got a hope in hell.'

'We're not in hell,' I had to tell him. 'We're in Number One Court at the Old Bailey. And there's always hope until the Jury comes back.'

'Of course you've got to say that. And of course you're putting up a great fight. But I've been looking at the Jury. They can't wait to sink you.'

'I'm not sure you're right,' I told the lawyer from the Arab world. 'I think I've got some friends on the Jury.'

'Oh, *her*.' He seemed to know exactly whom I meant. 'I don't think she's going to count much, is she? Sorry. Got to dash. I've got some calls to make before two o'clock.'

So he swept up his change from the counter, I saw a sun-browned hand, a wrist decorated with a discreetly expensive watch, a glittering cufflink, and he was gone, no doubt to make his calls and then climb back to the public gallery before I even had a chance of asking his name.

'I saw him at association. When we were watching the telly and what have you. In Brixton. I knew what he was in for, strangling the girl on Hampstead Heath, and most of them shunned him for it. He was very quiet usually. He just sat, not even looking at the telly. He seemed a lonely sort. So I sat near and spoke to him.'

'Did you become friendly?' Adrian Hoddinot was examining the witness whose evidence, arriving late as an afterthought, had seemed to strengthen the case against my client. Neville Skeate had apparently unburdened his soul and made a full confession to a fellow prisoner.

'I wouldn't say friendly. It was just that I thought he was the lonely sort. Needed a bit of cheering up. I'm the kind that will get along with anybody, so I engaged him in conversation.' William Phelps was a small, soft-eyed, untidy man who seemed only anxious to be liked. 'I think he appreciated that.'

He avoided, I noticed, looking at the man in the dock, although he had wanted to get on with him and engage him in conversation. For his part, Neville Skeate gazed upwards as though communicating with heavenly powers, and showed no sign of recognizing the friendly witness.

'Just tell us about any conversation you had with Skeate that might have been about this case.'

'What on earth does that mean?' I rose to object. '"*Might* have been about this case?" That would include my client telling this witness who was defending him.'

'I'm sure he did.' Adrian Hoddinot was languidly dismissive. 'My friend's name is pretty well known among the inmates of Brixton Prison.' He turned to the witness. 'Did he mention Hampstead Heath at all?'

'Don't lead,' I growled.

'Oh, very well.' Adrian gave the Jury a mock sigh, meaning, you can judge for yourselves the trouble I'm having with this old fart. 'Tell us if there's any conversation you can particularly remember.'

'There was a girl singer on the TV. Quite a good-looking girl, she was.'

'Is this relevant?' I rose to ask, but here the witness got the better of me. 'Oh yes it is, Mr Rumpole. Very relevant. He told me she looked a bit like that girl that he had to strangle on Hampstead Heath.'

'Did he say why he had to strangle her?' Adrian looked grateful to his witness.

'He didn't tell me that. He gave me no reason for it.'

'Thank you, Mr Phelps.' Adrian sat down then, having expressed, I thought, the sincere gratitude of the Crown Prosecution Service, the Metropolitan Police and the newspaper-reading public, who all wanted someone convicted for Pamela's death and now had a solid piece of evidence to achieve the longed-for result.

'Mr Phelps, are you telling this Jury that Neville Skeate confessed to murder as you and a number of other prisoners sat around watching television?' I waded in at the deep end.

'That's right. It seemed the sight of that girl reminded him.'

'You mean, otherwise he might have forgotten? How many other prisoners heard him?'

'I don't think no one heard. He spoke very low, you see. Just to me alone.'

'Just you alone? So we can take it you were the only witness to this conversation?'

'Just me that heard it, yes.'

'And you've had a pretty eventful career, haven't you, Mr Phelps, in and out of prison?'

'I've been in a bit of trouble and what have you, yes.'

'What have I? What have *you*, Mr Phelps.' I picked up the list of previous convictions and held it high so that the Jury could see that I had it all down on paper. 'Four sentences for fraud. Four for obtaining money by false pretences. Obtaining a false document with intent to deceive. And now you're in Brixton, awaiting trial on a charge of the fraudulent conversion of a vast quantity of frozen food ordered by you on credit for a restaurant that was discovered not to exist.'

'I'm defending that one.' He seemed proud of the fact.

'Then I wish you luck!' Kathleen Brewster liked that and gave me a small, congratulatory giggle. I even noticed other smiles on the hostile Jury faces. 'So it comes to this, doesn't it?' I went on. 'Time and time again you have been proved, beyond reasonable doubt, to be a fraud and a swindler.'

'If you like to put it that way.'

'Oh I do like to put it that way. I like to make it clear to this Jury that my client's so-called confession depends on the words of a convicted liar.'

'He said it!' By now I thought it safe to ignore the witness's protest.

'And a scoundrel.'

'I honestly did hear him say it.'

'Honestly? I would suggest to you, Mr Phelps, that you have very little idea of what that word means.'

'I told you what I heard, and I'm sticking to it.' If Mr Phelps had been a girl I would have said he pouted.

'Oh, you've got to stick to it, haven't you?'

'What do you mean? I've "got to".'

'This is a case where the police are desperate for a conviction. The only trouble is that they haven't got much evidence. Did anyone offer to go easy on your problem with the frozen food if you were kind enough to remember a convenient confession?'

The Jury were looking hard at Phelps, who seemed to be engrossed in a study of his shoes. There was a silence unhealthy for the prosecution which Adrian Hoddinot filled, doing his best to sound aggrieved.

'Is my learned friend suggesting a specific conversation with a particular officer?' Adrian Hoddinot got on his hind legs to object. 'If so, he should say so clearly to the witness.'

Of course I hadn't got a date to put or a name to name. 'No police officer has told me, "We managed to bribe the fraudster Phelps to say your man made a confession." I'm simply putting the possibility to the witness, my Lord. I think the Jury might be interested in his answer.'

The learned Beetle looked doubtful, then he turned his thick-lensed eyes on the Jury. They must have seemed to him to be very interested, so he told me I could ask my question.

I repeated it and Phelps raised his head and gave me a modest smile. 'They did mention my trial. Yes. When they took my statement they mentioned it.'

'What did they say exactly?'

'That they might go a bit easy on me. If I told them the truth about what Skeate said about the girl.'

Why did he say that? Did he imagine he'd find a way to make the Crown Prosecution Service stick to its bargain? Was he ashamed of grassing, even on so unattractive a character as Neville Skeate, or did he feel, as even proven liars sometimes do in the witness box, a sudden, irrational urge to tell the truth? Whatever it was, his answers had two immediate results. The smile on Number Four juror's face broadened considerably, and there was the sound of a slight disturbance in the public gallery as the sun-tanned, gold-watched, youngish lawyer from the Arab Emirates left in what seemed like a hurry.

When that day's proceedings were over, I was in an Old Bailey lift with Bonny Bernard when Number Four juror got in just as the doors were closing. Kathleen smiled at me, and I gave her a vague smile back. Then, to my horror, she opened her mouth and spoke. 'Mr Rumpole.'

'No!' I had to silence her. 'No, you mustn't! You can't possibly talk to me. I'll have to tell the Judge and . . . well, please don't.'

She turned away from me then and said no more. When the lift stopped we got out and went our separate ways in silence. But if I had listened to what she had to say it might have saved a good deal of trouble.

'You won't mind if I go out this evening, Rumpole?'

'Mind? Why should I mind?' The idea that She Who Must Be Obeyed would seek my agreement before embarking on any course of conduct was so novel that I must have looked surprised. 'Who are you going to meet? Someone you went to school with?' It usually was.

'No, Dermot Fletcher. You met Dermot, didn't you? At the Lysander Club. His wife's bunked off, he's got to report on a football match and the babysitter's not coming till later. I said I'd go over and hold the fort until she gets there. Little Tom, he's only six but a proper man. Always getting into trouble.' The way she said it made me feel vaguely inferior, as though I were not quite a proper man and didn't get into trouble enough, although, heaven knew, it wasn't for the want of trying. What was clear was that Hilda was looking forward far more eagerly to an evening with Tom than she would have with the shared shepherd's pie and television in my company. And yet I couldn't forget that surprising remark passed by Luci Gribble when she caught me on the stationary bicycle.

'By the way,' I tried to say it as casually as possible, 'exactly why do you want me to spend my time pedalling uselessly in the Lysander Club?'

'I told you, Rumpole.'

'I'm not sure you did.'

'I want you to lose weight.'

'That, of course.'

'To open your tubes and help your breathing. Make you sweat a little.'

'I know that. But didn't you have something else in mind? Some other . . .' I didn't want to put words in the witness's mouth, 'motive, perhaps?'

'I really don't know what you mean.' The witness was giving nothing away.

'Luci thought you might have had some other reason.'

'That Luci,' Hilda was not to be drawn further, 'doesn't know nearly as much as she thinks she does.' And then, after a silence, she repeated in a gentler tone, 'You're sure you don't mind if I go and look after little Tom?'

'Of course not. I'll be out this evening anyway. I'm going lap dancing.'

'Don't be silly, Rumpole.' She was looking at me with pity. 'You've used that joke before and it wasn't even funny the first time.'

Hilda was right. Whatever else you might say about lap dancing, it wasn't funny. If you were looking for laughs, they were more likely to be found listening to Soapy Sam Ballard discussing his triumphs before the Rent Tribunals in Pommeroy's than in the solemn precincts of the Candy Crocodile. The impression I got from the evening was of watching some perfectly pleasant and physically fit young women giving an exhibition of advanced gymnastics. All of which is not to say that my evening out with the lap dancers wasn't useful. Its use was vital and unexpected.

It had been Bonny Bernard who suggested it. 'I reckon we should do a bit of research one evening,' he had said, 'round that Candy Crocodile club.'

'It might be an idea,' I told him. 'There's something curiously unnerving about this case. I've got a friend in the Jury and a fan in the public gallery, and she keeps looking at him, but not as though she likes him very much. Apart from that, what are we meant to think? That Neville Skeate waited about on Hampstead Heath in the faint hope that the Whore of Babylon would come strolling along so he could strangle her? There's too much we can't explain. I suppose we might learn something in this Candy Crocodile.'

'You mean we should inspect the locus?' Bernard was, even for him, unusually enthusiastic. 'I don't suppose you'll want to be bothered with it, will you, Mr Rumpole?'

'Perhaps,' I was giving the matter careful consideration, 'I should join you. The girls she worked with might know something.'

'I should think so.' My instructing solicitor seemed to be in complete agreement. 'I should think they must know quite a lot.'

Darkness. Throbbing music. The almost complete absence of conversation. These were the things that greeted us as we sat down to our dinner in the Candy Crocodile. Then I noticed that Bonny Bernard was staring at a row of the sort of poles down which firemen slide rapidly when the alarms ring. Now scarcely dressed young women were climbing up and down such poles with little gasps of affection. We ordered fish and chips and my instructing solicitor, who had taken the trouble to check up on the rules of the establishment, outlined the programme ahead.

'You can get one to come over and dance for you, Rumpole. Then you give her ten pounds.'

'Just for dancing with us?'

'Not with us, Mr Rumpole. She dances by herself. You can

watch her, but absolutely no touching allowed. You understand that?'

'Of course. I certainly wouldn't touch.' It seemed odd,
though, and not the sort of prohibition I imagined existed in
Sodom and Gomorrah. Had our misguided client simply been
wasting his breath when he called for fire and brimstone to
destroy this apparently respectable eatery?

'Shall I ask one of them for a dance, Rumpole?'

'What I'd really like to ask for is a chat.'

It was odd how easily both requests could be satisfied.
Bernard sent a message by a waiter to a girl who, gripping the
fireman's pole between her thighs, was leaning back and
making flying motions with her arms. She arrived at our table
and gave her name as Christine. I congratulated her on her
gymnastic ability and asked if she had taken a course in
pole-dancing.

'No. Entirely self-taught.'

She slid out of what remained of her clothes and began to
dance in a sinuous manner for our benefit. With my usual
interest in fees, I discovered that Christine had to pay the
Candy Crocodile a hundred pounds for the pleasure of sliding
down one of the firemen's poles. She hoped to make that
back, and maybe double it, by requests to dance, not only, I
was sure, for a couple of lawyers in search of information.
Bernard told her that we were concerned in the Old Bailey
trial, without making it clear which side we were on.

'Terrible about Pamela. The girls all loved her. She was a
good friend to all of us.' Christine was undertaking a complicated series of gyrations. 'She and I had a lot in common.'

'What, exactly?' I asked her.

'The contemporary dance theatre. Pam and I both worked
on the fringe. You might have caught my *Mother Courage* at
the Bricklayers' Arms in Kilburn? It was only a small part,

but I think I was quite effective. Did you see it?' She asked that of Bonny Bernard as she waved her behind, perfectly shaped and white as alabaster, in front of his eyes. For the moment he seemed lost for words, so I had to tell her we had, through intense pressure of work, missed all the best things in the theatre lately.

'Too bad.' She spun round to face me. 'So you missed Pamela in *Dr Faustus*?'

'I'm afraid so. But talking of Pamela –'

'Poor Pam!'

'I just wonder about her son. Is he all right?'

'Cameron? Oh, he's great. He'll be a terrific guitarist.'

'There's someone to look after him?'

'Absolutely. A good friend of Pam's. An older woman, very responsible. She loves Cameron.' Christine did a sudden twist, her hands fondling her breasts, and smiled at the riveted Bonny Bernard. 'And he loves her.'

'So that's all right?'

'It will be as long as no one tries to take him away.'

'Is anyone likely to?'

'Some father Cameron's got somewhere. Pam was always afraid he'd try to take Cameron. Nice talking to you. I've got to go.'

The music had grown louder. Bernard handed Christine a ten-pound note, which she slipped neatly into the garter on her bare thigh. Then she was gone, back to slither down the fireman's pole and wait for another customer.

We finished our fish and chips. Bonny Bernard decided to invest in another dancer and I set off, through the darkness and with the music pounding in my ears, in search of the Gents'.

Outside the dining and dancing area, I encountered a maze of shadowy corridors, with lines of unmarked doors. Growing desperate, I pulled open one of them, hoping to strike lucky or at least find someone to ask. I saw no gleaming porcelain and heard no trickling water, all I saw was an untidy, ill-lit room. There was a table full of loaded ashtrays, half-emptied glasses and bits and pieces of abbreviated costumes. Two girls, taking time off, were huddled into sweaters, smoking busily and chatting to another, older woman. She was sitting beside a table lamp with a broken shade, stitching away at some minute article of clothing. At first her face was in the shadows, but as she raised her head to look, in considerable surprise, at me, I had no difficulty in recognizing her as Number Four in the Jury and my number-one fan.

Before I could ask a question, or even greet her, my arm was seized, and I was yanked back into the passage by a muscular-looking, crop-headed bouncer who had even less appeal than the witness Phelps. He slammed the door and, when I told him I was only looking for the loo, jerked a thumb towards the other side of the passage and grunted, I thought unnecessarily, 'On your way, peeping Tom. And don't do any more wandering.'

'Kathleen Brewster!'

No answer. The Clerk of the Court called again, and, once again, answer came there none. The clerk raised his head, saw the empty number-four place and called her name once more, as though she might have been loitering, gossiping behind some door. But no Kathleen came bustling in, smiling apologetically and then sitting down and looking around as though she'd been waiting a long time and wondered why we didn't all get on with it.

Now the clerk was talking to the Judge, probably telling him that no message from Kathleen had been received. I looked up at the public gallery and, as I had somehow suspected, the seat in the front row was empty. The sun-tanned stranger had vanished. Now the assiduous Beetle began the slow process of dealing with the case of a vanished juror. His first thought, naturally, was to adjourn so that we could all drink coffee and await events.

Adrian Hoddinot went up to discuss such legally important matters as fly fishing and deer stalking with fellow animal-lovers in the Bar Mess. I went to the public canteen, a place which smelled strongly of furniture polish and yesterday's hot dinners, in the hope of finding the officer in charge of the case alone and accessible to a bit of well-intentioned advice.

I was lucky; Detective Superintendent Leeming sat at a table with a cup of coffee, carefully unwrapping a KitKat, and seemed grateful for my company.

'Typical, isn't it, Mr Rumpole? People don't even take Jury duty seriously any more.'

'I'm not sure.' I slurped coffee and longed to light a small cigar. Sadly, the Old Bailey canteen had also been designated a smoke-free zone. 'Perhaps there are some things in life that are even more important than Jury service.'

'What do you mean by that?' Leeming paused in the unwrapping of his KitKat. He was a fairly plump officer with a cheerful expression, even when concerned with the most tragic and horrifying crimes. He liked nothing better than press conferences, where he could appear before the television cameras and hint at sensational knowledge which he wasn't yet at liberty to impart and extraordinary developments which were also, for the moment, under wraps.

'I just mean,' I was anxious to feed his curiosity, 'that there might be some surprising news for you to announce to the press. And I could possibly suggest a lead to the vanishing juror.'

'You've said nothing to the press about this as yet?' Leeming was worried.

'I came to you first, naturally.'

'Very wise, Mr Rumpole. Very wise of you indeed to cooperate with us. Surprising news, you say?'

'That might fill tomorrow's headlines.'

'Go on then, Mr Rumpole. Tell me more.' He bit into his KitKat then, as though looking forward to an even more nourishing feast of publicity.

So I told him where I thought he should look, and who he should look for, as soon as possible. He should, I thought, find the missing juror and much else besides.

'We might have something to announce at a press conference, do you think, Mr Rumpole?'

'I think you might have quite a lot to announce at a press conference.'

Some time later, when delays on the Tube had been accounted for and Kathleen's home number had provided no answer, the Beetle summoned us back into Court and, in the absence of the rest of the Jury, asked if we would agree to go on with a mere eleven good and honest citizens. Adrian Hoddinot, who now seemed desperately anxious to get the whole distressing business over, as he had, he told me, a far more lucrative disputed claim on an insurance company starting on Monday, agreed to dispense with my favourite juror.

'You have no objection to that, have you, Mr Rumpole?' The Beetle's eyes swivelled on to me.

'Yes I have, my Lord. A most serious objection.'

'Perhaps you'd let us know what it is?'

'She's the only person in the Jury box who's at all likely to vote for my client,' was what I couldn't say. Instead I told the Beetle, 'That particular juror has listened most attentively throughout the case. Indeed, she may well have been more attentive, and have the facts more clearly in mind, than most of the other jurors. It would be a great pity to lose her services because of some minor accident or misunderstanding which may be cleared up by tomorrow morning.'

'It may be.' The Beetle looked doubtful. 'Or it may not.'

'Besides which,' I added for good measure, 'I understand that the police are making certain enquiries today which may have fruitful results.'

'Enquiries relating to the missing juror?'

'I understand so, my Lord.'

'Is that so?' the Beetle asked Adrian, who consulted Detective Superintendent Leeming, who whispered a confirmation. Counsel for the Prosecution looked disappointed. His prospects of being free to do a serious money brief on Monday seemed to be fading by the minute.

'I understand there are enquiries being made today, my Lord,' he agreed, 'as Mr Rumpole has suggested.'

'Very well, then. Ten-thirty tomorrow morning. But if there's no further news of Miss Brewster then,' the Judge was determined, 'we'll have to go on with the remaining eleven.'

So there was a short stay of execution, during which much had to be revealed. I hadn't told the Beetle a particularly cogent reason for wanting a delay. The month was April and, although we were back at work at the Old Bailey, it was still the school holidays.

What happened that day at the basement flat in West Heath Road where Pamela McDonnell had lived in happiness with her son Cameron had nothing further to do with me. All I had done was to point DS Leeming in what I hoped was the right direction, and await results.

Kathleen Brewster, I had discovered from the Jury list, lived in Reddington Gardens, only a short walk from Pamela's flat

in West Heath Road. Kathleen worked at home on trans-
lations from and into French, which, it seemed, she spoke
fluently. She was also an addict of fringe theatre, and had met
Pam at a party in the venue over a pub in Kilburn. She had
got to know Cameron and, having no children of her own,
took to him greatly. It was she who gave him French lessons,
his guitar lessons being in the hands of the elderly member of
a once successful rock group who lived in Childs Hill.

Kathleen had spent the night before her disappearance
from the Jury in West Heath Road, where she had put
Cameron to bed. Early in the morning, however, the phone
rang and a man's voice announced briskly that he was
Cameron's father and he would be round to collect his son at
midday. He wanted Cameron's clothes packed and the boy
ready to travel. If there were things that couldn't be easily
transported they would be sent for later. The man had then
rung off, as though he was in a considerable hurry and
expected his instructions to be carried out to the letter.

Kathleen was in a panic. She remembered Pam telling her
about Cameron's father, a man with an uncontrollable temper
and given to violence, who rarely appeared, but when he did
often threatened to take his son away from a 'world of tarts,
ponces and gay actors' to join him abroad, where the boy
would have 'a chance of mixing with some decent people' and
might be able to look forward to 'a job with a future in an oil
company'. None of these threats had come to anything, but
shortly before her death Pamela had heard from a mutual
friend that Cameron's father was about to get married and
start a new home in the Middle East. This might, she had
told Kathleen, be good news or bad. It would be good if he
wanted to acquire a new family and so would forget about
Cameron, bad if he wanted Cameron to join him in a new
home with a new wife.

No one had been with Pamela on the night she died. She had put Cameron to bed and that was the last time he had seen his mother. Somehow she must have left the boy sleeping, gone out for a walk on the Heath and met her terrible death. It seemed an extraordinary coincidence when Kathleen was summoned to Jury service and found herself as one of the judges of fact in her friend's murder trial. All I can tell you is that such coincidences are not unknown. It's enough to say that she had her suspicions about Pam's murderer, and such suspicions didn't include Neville Skeate, the Ninth Day Elamite. For this reason, and this reason alone, she didn't want Neville convicted. She smiled at me because she feared the guilt lay elsewhere, not, I'm afraid, because she was overcome by the charm and power of my advocacy.

But on that morning when Cameron was to be taken from her, Kathleen Brewster forgot the trial. She had no time to worry about her failure to appear in the Jury box. She phoned Dick Catford, the ageing guitarist, and Christine, who had got home at four a.m. from the Candy Crocodile but was glad to be called up for the protection of Pam's son. Kathleen also rang the local police, warning them of the proposed abduction of a child. The weary voice listening to her at first said it was a matrimonial dispute with which the police couldn't become concerned. Later she was able to get in touch with another department, which promised to send a social worker, who never arrived. Cameron was collected by another friend from the Candy Crocodile, who offered to take him for lunch at McDonald's and then to *The Lord of the Rings* at the Odeon Swiss Cottage. Short of nailing up the doors and borrowing a shotgun, Kathleen and her friends felt they could do no more.

Access to Pam's flat was to be discovered down a dark and slippery flight of steps from the front of a large Edwardian house. A door in the area led into her basement flat. At a quarter to twelve, Christine and Dick the guitarist were waiting behind an open bedroom door, while Kathleen stood bravely by the entrance. At exactly twelve o'clock a man came down the steps into this area.

She opened the door to him, and he was exactly whom she had feared. The man she thought she might have been able to recognize from a half-forgotten photograph Pam had once showed her, the man she had sat opposite in Court and had looked up at ever since the trial began. He was the man with the helmet of fair hair and the fashionable suit, the brilliant cufflinks and the expensive watch, and, as I couldn't help noticing when he picked up his change from the pub counter, the large and powerful hands.

What happened then became the subject of witness statements and depositions, and some of the words may have been challenged, confused and misremembered. But I'm certain that the man, the father, asked if Cameron was ready to go, and sure that Kathleen told him that the boy wasn't there and wouldn't be handed over. At which the well-dressed, up to then quietly spoken lawyer with a Middle Eastern oil company was maddened with rage. He shouted, and what he shouted was clearly audible to the waiting witnesses in the bedroom. 'She wouldn't agree to let me have him. And you know what happened to her! She said she'd stop him leaving the country. You want a bit of the same, do you?' His face was distorted with fury, the face that Pam had seen for a last time when, helpless with rage and frustration, he had taken her by the throat as they walked together on Hampstead Heath.

His hands were on Kathleen's neck when Christine and Dick the guitarist came down the passage towards him. He turned, and saw Detective Superintendent Leeming, with his Inspector and Sergeant, coming down the steps, and he dropped his hands. Surrounded by witnesses, he started on the long legal journey which ended in his taking Neville Skeate's place in the Old Bailey dock as the true killer of Pamela McDonnell.

'After he killed Pamela he went back abroad. It was only when he heard they'd arrested someone else he thought it was safe to come back to England. He took risks, of course he took risks. He turned up at the Old Bailey every day to make sure that the Ninth Day Elamite was convicted. It was when I'd cross-examined the Brixton grass that he thought Neville might, just possibly, be acquitted. So he decided to grab his son and shoot back to the Arab Emirates.'

'But why did Mrs Brewster want to meet at the flat? She'd sent the boy away. Why didn't she just stay clear of the whole business?'

'I think she hoped he'd give himself away. She wanted him out of Cameron's life for a long time. She'd decided to solve the mystery of Pamela's death. And she felt there was something in life more important, even, than Jury service.'

'What do you mean, Rumpole?

'I'm talking about a child. A young boy, accomplished on the guitar, whose father had killed his mother. I think Kathleen would have done anything for him. Of course, she wanted Neville Skeate to get off during the trial, so the real murderer could be convicted. She should have left that to Rumpole.'

'Nonsense! You told me you thought you were on a loser.'

'That's what Cameron's father hoped. But I disappointed him. No one should ever underestimate Rumpole, when he's doing a murder alone and without a leader.'

But Hilda had lost her unusual interest in my work and she was smiling at some other thought. 'I'm afraid I'll be out again this evening.'

'Let me guess. Young Tom needs a babysitter?'

'He's so clever. He calls me Mrs Rumpy!'

Is that a sign of high intellectual attainment, I wondered? But of course I didn't say it. I said, 'Don't worry, I'll be perfectly all right.'

'You won't make that joke about lap dancing again, will you, Rumpole?'

'No, Hilda. Never again.'

My lap-dancing days were over, and I tried to keep any note of regret from my voice.

After the long legal process ahead, Neville Skeate was liberated, but I never heard that he returned to the Candy Crocodile. I believe his voice was still heard from time to time at various other sinks of iniquity, condemning London to destruction by fire and brimstone. But his abuse had become quieter, his fellow Elamites had drifted away, and life in our city of the plain went on unrepentant.

Rumpole Redeemed

'By the way, Rumpole, have you been keeping up with your exercises at the Lysander Club?' The cross-examination started, as the best do, in a quiet and casual manner; but I sniffed danger.

'Of course,' I answered boldly and then, to cover myself, added, 'whenever I get the chance.'

'So what is it that stops you going regularly?'

'Pressure of work.' I kept it vague, but hoped that would settle the matter.

'Oh yes?' Hilda sounded unconvinced. 'I thought I heard you complain about the shortage of work lately, the rare appearance of briefs. And yet Dermot Fletcher tells me he never sees you on the bicycle!'

I quietly cursed the grey-haired sports commentator whose small boy had become Hilda's favourite person. Weren't there football matches, had cricket been abandoned so that this man could spend his life noticing my absence from the stationary bicycle?

'I get round to the Lysander whenever I can.' It was time to call my best evidence. 'If you look at the book you'll see I'm signed in.'

'I have looked at the book. And I've seen you signed in by Luci Gribble. Perhaps you'd be good enough to tell me how many times you went to the club with Luci?'

'Off and on. Look, I'd better be getting down to Chambers. See what's around. I believe Henry's got me a dangerous driving.'

'Don't prevaricate, Rumpole.' It was a word Hilda's father had liked to use in Court; I suppose he sometimes took it home with him. At least she didn't say 'Don't fence with me!' 'I have spoken to Luci Gribble.'

That was it, then. I stood and watched my defence collapse like a tent in a tornado.

'I have spoken to Luci Gribble,' Hilda repeated, 'and she had to admit that on most of the occasions when you asked her to sign you in, you didn't join her. You were notably absent, Rumpole, but no doubt shortening your life over-dosing on red wine in that favourite wine bar of yours.'

'Can I change my plea?' I took a quick legal decision. 'Guilty.'

'Of course you are. What can we do about you, Rumpole?' she sighed heavily. My case was clearly hopeless.

'I can only say,' I started to mitigate, 'I do find bicycling nowhere to Caribbean music, even with an occasional word from your friend the sports commentator, deeply boring.'

'Boring? Oh, I'm so sorry.' Hilda had now adopted the retort contemptuous. 'I'm sorry I can't provide a few murders, or a bank robbery, or a nice long fraud to keep you entertained, Rumpole. You can't live entirely for pleasure. You've got to put up with a bit of boredom occasionally, if you want to keep yourself alive. So it's entirely up to you. I can no longer take any responsibility for you.'

At which she left the kitchen where breakfast, together with much else, was over. Shortly after that I heard the sound of angry hoovering from the sitting-room. My case of non-compliance with exercise requirements was clearly lost and I was free to go.

★

Aware that a chill wind of disapproval would be blowing round Froxbury Mansions that evening, I delayed my homeward journey by a brief visit to the wine bar Hilda had condemned in her judgement. I wandered into Pommeroy's as lonely as a cloud, and was accompanied only by a single glass of Château Fleet Street when I heard a brisk, upper-crust voice at my elbow. 'Rumpole! I want to invite you to lunch.'

'Then invite, old darling.'

I gave Archie Prosser full permission to feed me, regardless of expense. The newest arrival in our Chambers in Equity Court, Prosser was a distant relative of Lord someone or other, an obscure link which predisposed She Who Must Be Obeyed slightly in his favour. Soapy Sam Ballard had introduced him into Chambers as a sparkling wit, one likely to set Pommeroy's Wine Bar in a roar, but I hadn't yet heard him utter any line, or produce any thought worth including in a slim volume to be entitled *The Wit and Wisdom of Archie Prosser*. He was, however, an inoffensive soul who had been cooperative when he prosecuted me in the case of the female Fagin of the Underground. He was also, as he was continuously reminding me, a member of the Sheridan Club, a somewhat gloomy and ill-lit institution which does, as Archie was fond of telling us all, an excellent liver and bacon, which, if preceded by nine oysters in the half shell and followed by a summer pudding well covered with cream, the whole to be washed down with some rare vintage never even heard of in Pommeroy's, might make Archie seem an agreeable companion for lunch and the smoking of an unusually large cigar. In return, I could reward him with a few of my jokes which had, like the wine, improved with age.

'Delighted,' I told him. 'Any time next week would suit me. I think I may have what Luci Gribble would call a window of opportunity. There's been a rise in the law-abiding rate. I think it's hitting everybody.'

Not much of a joke, I agree, and Archie took it without a smile. Instead he gave me a look of deep and maddening concern. 'I bet you're glad of the rest, aren't you, Rumpole?'

At this my patience snapped. 'No,' I told him. 'I'm not in the least glad of the rest. I'm bored to tears by the rest. I've had quite enough rest to last until my final day on earth, which I intend to spend wearing a wig and arguing. I just wanted to point out that, as luck would have it, I've got one of Luci's windows next week and I'd be delighted to fill it with a lengthy lunch at your club.'

'You mean the Sheridan?'

'Of course I mean the Sheridan.'

'Talking of which,' Archie told me, 'I'm going to put Bernard up for membership. I think he'd appreciate that, don't you?'

'Bonny Bernard? You're speaking of my favourite solicitor. I feel sure he would. And I'm equally sure I'd enjoy lunch with you there. Very kind of you, Archie.'

'I'm afraid I wasn't thinking exactly in terms of the Sheridan.'

'All right, if you insist. Where were you thinking in terms of?' I imagined Archie Prosser's ideas had gone upmarket. 'The Ritz?'

'Not exactly, Rumpole.' The unpredictable Archie seemed to be shaking with some particular private joke. 'I was thinking more in terms of Worsfield Prison.'

We lived in a time when the Government was cracking down on everything. Every week, it seemed, brought a new list of things which were to be cracked down on: single mothers who didn't make sure their children went into school, noisy neighbours, graffiti artists and mobile-phone stealers were to be cracked down on with particular severity. What was noticeable was that very little was cracked up. There was a total absence of Government announcements offering a free glass of Guinness on the National Health and wishing everyone a good time. The cracking down had become so universal that I didn't know when I would wake up to discover that Château Thames Embankment, small cigars and legal jokes more than three years old were being cracked down on, and that I was on my way to Worsfield and not just for lunch.

Another dearly held belief of the puritan masters of what claimed to be a deeply caring political party was that prison was a universal panacea. Like a magic potion which could relieve headaches, tonsillitis, yellow fever and broken legs, prison could do you nothing but good. The result of all this cracking down and locking up was that the prison population had risen to record levels, the nicks were bursting at the seams, the mad and bad were packed in with the merely muddled. In the face of this wave of overcrowding the Bunyan Society (named after a devout and imprisoned author) stood like Canute. It published facts and figures, protesting at the incarceration of fifteen-year-olds, the absence of education, the failure to stop reoffending and the sad story of a women's prison without a visitors' lavatory, where friends and relatives were instructed to pee in the car-park hedge. Ministers received these reports politely, perhaps even read them, and continued to crack down as before. The Bunyan Society's reply was to arrange, so Archie Prosser told me, a lunch in Worsfield Prison, outside London, where the great and the good could show their solidarity with those of my customers whom even the Rumpole magic touch couldn't save from custody.

'Now I'm on the Committee of the Bunyan Society.' Archie

Prosser announced the fact with some satisfaction, feeling no doubt that he'd joined the great and the good. 'I suggested we should have a representative of the old-fashioned criminal defender present at our prison lunch. You'll be at home, Rumpole. I'm sure you'll know lots of the people there.'

'Yes,' I agreed and there was, I'm afraid, a mournful note in my voice, 'I most probably will.'

'This way! Would you mind looking this way?'

'Over here. Over on your right for the *Daily Post*.'

'Look at me now. No – me, not him. All right. That's lovely!'

These were voices behind flashes of light as I approached, in drizzling rain, the castellated mini towers that flanked the gates of Worsfield Prison. When the flashes were no longer blinding me I saw, among the men with cameras, the shadowy figure of Luci Gribble, our Chambers Director of Marketing, wearing a white belted mackintosh and a smile of achievement.

'Well done, Horace! That's a great photo opportunity!'

I was about to say 'Opportunity for what?' when one of the photographers asked her, 'Who the hell was he?'

'Counsel for the defence,' Luci told him. 'Just an ordinary, everyday criminal barrister. An old workhorse paying a visit to his clients. Not a leader, perhaps, but one of the trusted foot soldiers of our Chambers at Equity Court. No, not Rumbold. Rumpole. R–U–M . . .'

Times have changed. When I joined our Chambers, in Hilda's father's time, you would have been threatened with dismissal and heavily fined if you'd allowed your photograph to appear in a newspaper. Now we were being packaged and advertised like Cornflakes. There was no chance of arguing about it with Luci. It was lunchtime and the old workhorse was in search of its nosebag. I rang a bell set into the stonework and a screw appeared with a bunch of jangling keys attached. 'Name please?' he said, consulting a list. I had never felt more anonymous.

The menu featured grey mince, watery mashed potatoes, digestive biscuits and a blue plastic mug of tepid water. The tables were set out in a main assembly area, and at each one, a member of the great and the good shared the feast with representatives of the small and the iffy. I sat between two thieves, one about to be set loose once more on the fallible locks and vulnerable window fastenings of the outside world. The other, once of the same persuasion, was so redeemed that he now worked for the Bunyan Society, gave lectures to gatherings of sociologists, students of criminology and interested police officers, and had sold his autobiography, *Set a Thief*, to a publisher. His name, proudly announced on the Bunyan Society label pinned to his jacket, was Brian Skidmore. He was a pale-faced fellow, probably in his early forties, with a high, aquiline nose which gave him the inappropriate look of a medieval cleric, and a case of premature baldness which added to the monkish nature of his appearance. He introduced the soon-to-be-released prisoner. 'This is Chirpy Molloy. I don't know if you've ever bumped into him round the Courts, Mr Rumpole.' Brian sounded like a schoolteacher introducing the most hopeless but likeable member of the class.

'You were never my brief, were you, Mr Rumpole?' I could see why he was called Chirpy. He was small, round-faced, plump, and his smile, half challenging, half defensive, must have stayed with him since he was a bright-eyed, tousle-headed child always responsible for the broken window, the fight in the playground or the missing contribution for the school outing.

'I never had that pleasure.' I bit into a digestive biscuit; it went badly with the mince.

'Me being a Molloy, and you always appearing on behalf of the Timsons.'

He was speaking of one of the great divides. The Montagues and the Capulets were friendly neighbours compared to the Timsons and the Molloys. This particular Molloy, however, was held even by the Timsons to be a perfectly straightforward and strictly non-violent villain, who appeared to his pub acquaintances and to the juries who were called on to try him to be a cheerful Cockney chappie who could take the rough with the smooth, the benefit of the doubt with the guilty verdict, and the big blow-outs in a Marbella holiday hotel with the grey mince and biscuits in Worsfield.

'We Molloys generally use Mr Arkwright in Queen Alexandra's Buildings. You heard of him?'

'Of course I know Percy Arkwright. I believe, as a defender, he's a great help to the prosecution.' I shouldn't have said it, but grey mince does bring out the worst in people.

'You mean I'd be better off with you, Mr Rumpole?'

'Perhaps. If you consult Mr Bernard, solicitor of Camberwell, he'd lead you to me.'

'I'd say I'll remember that for next time,' Chirpy was now looking extra cheerful, 'but there's not going to be a next time. I'm sure of that.'

'Chirpy has decided to go straight, Mr Rumpole.' Brian Skidmore was once again the schoolteacher, announcing, in an amused sort of way, that one of his less talented pupils was planning to build, in the carpentry lesson, a light aircraft capable of transatlantic flight.

'To be honest, I got a girlfriend, and she doesn't like me being away in prison, Mr Rumpole. She's always on about it. She says she gets lonely nights. I've got to listen to her. I'm going to get a job round her father's Videos R Us and that'll be the end of it.'

'You mean you're going to buy your own aftershave from now on, Chirpy?' Brian was gently mocking.

Now I remembered what the Timsons had told me, with considerable amusement, about Chirpy Molloy. He was devoted to personal hygiene. He chose fairly small but expensive houses to break into, places belonging to owners who were known to be away on holiday. After collecting whatever valuables he could find, he invariably treated himself to a long and luxurious session in the bathroom. He sprinkled bath salts from glass jars into deep, hot water. He made considerable use of the Imperial Leather soap and applied the loofah. He borrowed the electric razor, slapped on the stinging perfume of Pour Les Hommes or Machisimo by Peruque. He didn't spare the hand cream or the all-over body lotion. Then he would dress again in his working clothes and, having wiped off all possible fingerprints, make a dignified exit through a back door. The bathroom, after he left it, looked as though it had been hit by a typhoon. He needn't have bothered about the fingerprints, the laughing Timsons told me, he might as well have left his name and address on the hall table.

'It's a wise decision,' I was telling Chirpy. 'If you've got a good job and a good girlfriend you certainly don't need me!'

'Quiet, Rumpole.' Archie Prosser gave me orders from the next table. 'The Home Secretary is about to say a few words.' And he added, as though to remind me of one of the highlights of my long life, 'You *have* met her. Don't you remember?'

Of course I remembered Bunty Heygate, the elegant but earnest Minister in the Home Office. I had met her with Archie in the Sheridan Club when I was engaged in the case of Doctor Nabi, an asylum seeker. She had been arguing that such colourful customs as cutting off hands, or stoning

women to death for adultery, were traditional in certain countries, and that it would be racist to denounce them, and
unreasonable to protect those who were in flight from them.
Such views must have found favour with the Government, as
Bunty had, in the latest reshuffle, been promoted to Home
Secretary, in which office she had forsaken her nickname and
announced that she would, from now on, be known as Brenda.

So there she was in all her glory, smiling with an even
deeper self-satisfaction now she was a Secretary of State. She
still looked, however, like an enormously successful schoolgirl
who had suddenly found herself promoted to headmistress.
The page-boy haircut was neat and burnished, she was wearing a bottle-green suit, and her high-heeled, pointed-toed
shoes clicked across the stone floor as she found the most
favourable speaking position. Above her, galleries of cells rose
like a great circle in a theatre; a net was stretched beneath the
top one to catch any long-term convicts who might be tempted
to take a quick way out. Brenda Heygate's clear, untroubled
voice carried easily, not only to the furthest visitor but to the
lifers far above her.

'It's a great pleasure to be here,' she said, 'and to share
with so many of you this excellent prison meal.' Was mine
the only muted groan? 'I have to say, on behalf of all of us in
Government, and in particular those of us in the Home Office,
that we are profoundly grateful to the Bunyan Society for
(here she seemed to have some trouble remembering exactly
what it was she was grateful to the Bunyan Society for, so she
retreated, as soon as possible, to her familiar territory) – for
the very useful work it has done, and, of course, for organizing
this get-together. Now, I'm sure we'll all have read in today's
papers I have made an important announcement.' The
inmates looked at her blankly, being unlikely to have read
Home Office pronouncements, and the great and the good

supporters of the Bunyan Society let out a disappointed sigh. 'We have, as you know, greatly improved the safety on our streets and reduced the crime rate since the opposition party were in power and old people were in genuine fear of taking a short walk down to the corner shop. However, there is one area in which the crime rate is, unfortunately, rising, and this is what I have called "Short-break burglary". This is when criminals find that the householder is taking, shall we say, a short break in Paris, or perhaps Barcelona, or enjoying a longer break during school holidays, and takes advantage.' (Here I glanced at Chirpy Molloy, who was looking modestly down at his plate as the Home Secretary discussed his special subject.) 'We have issued a Home Office warning to everyone going away for a holiday not to advertise the fact by cancelling, shall we say, the milk, or the daily papers. A sensible idea would be to donate your milk and papers to a friendly neighbour during a holiday period. Meanwhile, I give you all fair warning that I mean to crack down heavily on short-break burglaries, the maximum sentence for which will be seven years, which I hope to see applied in appropriate cases. Unlike the previous party in power, we intend to wake up the judiciary, who seem to find it a little difficult to move with the times, and make them crack down appropriately.

'Finally, I'd like to say that, at this excellent lunch, we have, thanks to the Bunyan Society, a remarkable proof of what we have always said – that prison can work and does work in many cases. I'm going to ask Brian Skidmore to say a few words to you.' It seemed to have been the usual story. 'Brian came from a broken home and lacked the role model of a father figure.' Here it was the turn of Brian Skidmore to look down modestly at his plate. 'He turned to minor crime as a youth, and then got into more serious trouble, but it was here at Worsfield that a few words from the Governor made the great change in his life. Now, as I'm sure you know, he works full time for the Bunyan Society and has kept completely out of trouble. Inmates of Worsfield and their guests, will you all welcome Brian Skidmore! Come along Brian, don't be shy!'

Although he said, 'Excuse me, Mr Rumpole. I never wanted anything like this,' Brian didn't seem in the least shy. In a surprisingly short time he was up beside the Home Secretary and was greeted, as an ex-prisoner, by warmer applause from the great and the good.

'I'm not used to this,' he said. 'This is worse than a prison sentence, having to speak. All I can say is I have to thank a lot of people. First of all, Mr Frank Dalton, when he was Governor. I was up on a charge for something, and he said, "Why don't we see you in chapel, Skidmore? There's something we get to learn there. Do you know what that is?" Well, of course I didn't know whatever he was talking about, and when I heard what they read out from the Bible I wasn't any the wiser. The words were "The Redemption of their soul is precious." I didn't know what redemption was in those days, but I do now. Because Mr Dalton explained it. We could all get off the crime if we tried hard enough. With a bit of help we could. So he arranged to put me in touch with the Bunyan Society. They were visiting here at the time, and they gave me a job, making the tea, mostly. And now I'm under-manager in charge of events. So thanks for coming and a special vote of thanks, for agreeing to fit us into her busy schedule, to the Home Secretary.'

At which the crackers-down and the cracked-down-on applauded. The party was breaking up when Archie Prosser suddenly said the word 'Applethorpe!' and started pushing his way between the departing guests towards a distant table, where a small, slightly wizened prisoner was thoughtfully picking his teeth.

Meanwhile, Chirpy had gone smiling back to his cell. 'He'll never make it, you know.' The redeemed Brian Skidmore had come back to our table and was watching Chirpy's retreat with pity and some amusement.

'Never make what?' I asked him.

'Never go straight. Not poor old Chirpy. He'll leave here with no money and probably no job. No one to look after him.'

'What about the girlfriend? And her father's Videos R Us?'

'She hasn't bothered to wait for him. That's what I heard in the chat round here. Of course, Chirpy doesn't know that yet. He'll be the last to know. So I doubt the job's still open. He'll drift back to the Molloys and you know what that means.'

'I'm not sure that I do know exactly.'

'I'm afraid he'll be looking for a house where the milk's been cancelled because they've all gone on holiday.'

'You think Chirpy Molloy's incapable of redemption?'

'We can hope for the best.' Brian put on the serious expression he had used for his speech. 'We can always hope. But we've got to face the facts, Mr Rumpole. This is it. The facts have to be faced.'

I moved on then, towards freedom and, in the fullness of time, a glass with better stuff than tepid water in it. Archie Prosser joined me at the prison gates. 'Who the hell was Applethorpe?' I asked him.

'Poor chap.' Archie looked serious. 'I was at school with him. In here waiting to be sentenced for thirty-two cases of indecent exposure. Come to think of it, he was Head Boy.'

Since my abandonment of the stationary bicycle, and Hilda's discovery of the fraudulent entries in the Lysander Club's records, home life in Gloucester Road began to feel like an extended visit to the Worsfield nick. No cries of welcome greeted me when I returned to the mansion flat, no sighs of regret when I left it after a hurried breakfast. Archie had made me a member of the Bunyan Society and I took refuge in some of its meetings, where I got to know the committee and was greeted warmly by the reformed Brian Skidmore. He told me that Chirpy Molloy had been released, but there was no news as yet of his having slid back into a life of crime.

I was in my Chambers room, wondering when, if ever, a brief in a sensational new case would arrive, when Claude Erskine-Brown stole in, looked down the passage as though he feared listeners, and carefully closed the door.

'Rumpole, I don't know if you've heard any rumours?'

'Rumours? Of course I've heard rumours. Where do you think life in Chambers would be without rumours?'

'Well, if you've heard any, don't believe them.'

'Why ever not? I usually believe rumours. But so far as politicians are concerned, I never believe anything until it's been officially denied.'

'Politicians?' Claude looked startled and afraid. 'Did you say politicians, Rumpole?'

'That's what I said.'

'So then you've heard.' He sat down in my client's chair in an attitude of despondent resignation.

'Heard what, exactly, Erskine-Brown?'

'About me and – well – her. I knew it would leak out eventually.'

Here, I thought, we go again. Claude Erskine-Brown, unlike the blessed Brian Skidmore, appeared irredeemable. Love provided as irresistible a temptation to him as crime did to such weak-minded characters as Chirpy Molloy. The only difference was that Erskine-Brown's infidelities, unlike Chirpy's burglaries, tended to remain in the world of dreams. As I was taught by my old, blind law tutor at Keeble College, a crime requires a guilty act with a guilty intent. Dear old Claude had the guilty intent most of the time; it was the guilty act he found hard to pull off.

'There's only one thing I do beg of you, Rumpole. And I know I can count on you, because of our long friendship over the years.'

'You want a bit of free Legal Aid?'

'Not that. No. It hasn't come to that. It's just if you hear my name mentioned in connection with a well-known politician . . .'

I began to run them over in my mind. The Prime Minister? Leader of the Opposition? What on earth had come over poor old Claude? He couldn't resist, of course, supplying the answer. 'If you hear my name mentioned in connection with, for instance, the Home Secretary, just say you know there's absolutely nothing in it.'

'Erskine-Brown! *Not* the Home Secretary?' I couldn't believe it.

'You don't know her, Rumpole?'

'Indeed I do. She's a woman who believes that we shouldn't blame countries who stone women to death and she's very keen on cracking down on people. You want to be careful she doesn't crack down on you, Claude.'

The man in my armchair assumed a far-away 'if only' expression. Then came a low murmur. 'I had the privilege of sitting next to her at a dinner in the Law Society. We really hit it off. She told me she found me a witty and sympathetic companion.'

'Mrs Justice Erskine-Brown – that is to say Lady Phillida – she was at this dinner party, was she?'

'Oh no. Philly was away on circuit somewhere.'

'So the Home Secretary had you to herself?'

'Almost entirely. She talked to the man on the other side,

of course, but not for very long. I walked her to her car and she kissed me, Rumpole. I was kissed by a Secretary of State. And I kissed her back!'

'I suppose I ought to congratulate you.'

'It's the power, I suppose. There's a sort of potent sexuality about her.'

'I can't honestly say I noticed.'

'I've always thought she was terribly attractive in photographs, of course. But in the flesh! Well, now it's happened, we might meet at the Opera. Or a quiet dinner in a restaurant.'

'The possibilities are endless.'

'That's right, Rumpole! Of course, we'll have to be extremely careful. So do, please, just remember, this conversation never happened.' At which Claude left my client's chair and slunk off, on whatever business he had in hand.

It was a few days after this that an unfortunate event occurred at the home of Adele Alexander, the well-known actress, near Sloane Square. While she was away on a holiday in Majorca, her house, Number 5 Granville Road, was broken into and valuable jewellery was stolen. The remarkable thing, according to the police, was that the thief had enjoyed all the benefits of the bathroom: wet towels were left on the floor and a prodigious amount of bath salts and various lotions had been made use of.

I heard no rumours of Erskine-Brown's burgeoning love affair with the Home Secretary; but the member of the Timson family I was defending for dangerous driving told me that, as I had suspected, Chirpy Molloy had been arrested exactly a month after his release from Worsfield. 'It's the bath he can't resist,' young Les Timson told me. 'That's what's his undoing. That and the toilet requisites.' Clearly the doctrine of redemption didn't apply to Chirpy Molloy.

★

The period which followed the arrest of Chirpy Molloy for serial burglary and stolen jewellery was not, as I have already indicated, a golden age in the life of Rumpole. The sentence passed on me at home was clearly a long one and there was no hope of parole, or indeed any clear indication of when, or even if, I might expect a release. It would be an exaggeration to say that Hilda was silent when we were alone together, but she was, for most of the time, monosyllabic. Her longest speech, often repeated to the accompaniment of heavy sighs and upward glances, as though calling on the gods to witness her patience in the face of such outrageous persecution, was 'Of course, if you're looking for an early death, Rumpole, and can't be bothered to look after your health in any way, that's entirely up to you. Just don't expect *me* to do anything about it. That's all.' Having said this, she would leave to look after little Tom Fletcher, a child who no doubt exercised obediently, performing hand stands and vaulting over the furniture, so insuring many long and healthy years to come. My dinner, as often as not, had not been left in the oven.

I tried various ploys. I attempted washing up, but She examined the plates and glasses critically, under a strong light, and then washed them up all over again. I tried a legal joke or two, but got an even heavier sigh and 'Please, Rumpole, not *that* one again.' I brought her the latest gossip, the strange misunderstanding over Judge Bullingham's wig, the unfortunate e-mail Soapy Sam Ballard sent to our Director of Marketing, but failed to capture Hilda's interest. The only thing I felt unable to concede was to return to the misery of the exercise bicycle in the Lysander Health Club. The day of the treadmill was, I had made up my mind, over. So I opted for what almost amounted to solitary confinement in Froxbury Mansions.

To make matters worse, briefs, which in happier times had fallen as thick as autumn leaves in my space on the clerks' room mantelpiece, were still as rare as swallows in winter. Every morning, when I strolled into Chambers and asked Henry if there was anything much in the diary, he would say, 'Very little on at the moment, Mr Rumpole. I expect you'll be glad of the rest.' So I would retreat to my room to light a small cigar, struggle with *The Times* crossword or consider the possibility of writing my memoirs.

On one eventful morning, however, as I wandered into the clerks' room and glanced at the mantelpiece, I saw a brief clearly marked by the firm of Bernard and Tillbury of Cold-harbour Lane, Camberwell. I knew that Bonny Bernard wouldn't think of briefing anyone else in Chambers and I was interested to see whom the Queen, as the prosecuting party in all criminal trials, was after this time. The title of the case was none other than *R. v. Molloy*. Henry was out of the room on some mission of his own, so I grabbed the brief and carried it off to study at my leisure.

An hour later, I had not only read it but made a note of all the facts, together with a list of questions to be asked when we saw our client, no doubt a great deal less chirpy. After this welcome work, I lit a small cigar, leant back and blew what I flatter myself was a perfect smoke ring at the ceiling. The case seemed so obvious, the violation of the victim's bathroom so completely in character, that it was going to be difficult to think of a defence. And yet, I thought, and yet . . . I was lost in the sessions of sweet silent thought when the door burst open and I was rudely interrupted.

'So, Rumpole!' Archie Prosser seemed full of righteous indignation, as though he'd caught me red-handed pinching the small change for the coffee contributions. 'You've got the brief!'

'Yes, Archie,' I told him politely. 'Thanks to you.'

'What do you mean, "thanks to me"?'

'You took me to that ghastly lunch. That's when I met Chirpy Molloy. He said he'd remember me the next time he was in trouble. Well, it seems he's back in trouble extremely soon.'

'I have no idea what the defendant Molloy may or may not have said to you. All I know is that what you have there is *my* brief.'

'Your what?'

'Brief.'

'Don't babble, Archie. This case comes from my old friend Bonny Bernard.'

'My instructing solicitor.'

'*Yours?*' I couldn't believe it.

'You might take the trouble to look at the name on the front of those papers.'

I turned them over. It was true. I had read the name of the case and the solicitors, but now I saw in the small print the inexcusable name of the learned friend, Mr Archibald Prosser.

'Bonny Bernard,' I was struggling with the enormity of the idea, 'is briefing *you*?'

'He thought perhaps he should cast his net a little wider.'

'And pick up some rather odd fish,' was what I didn't say.

'Anyway, it's a pretty hopeless case.' Archie sat down in a more forgiving mood. 'Absolutely no defence, so far as I can see. Fellow couldn't resist using the bathroom. So he left his signature.'

'He told me he was going straight this time.'

'They all say that, don't they?'

'You don't believe in the possibility of redemption?'

'For people like Molloy, with a string of convictions as long as your arm? Hardly.'

I was putting back the papers, having decided to surrender them with as much gallantry as possible. 'I'll leave you my note. There are one or two things you might consider. Was it pretty widely known, for instance, that this actress was in the habit of leaving jewellery around when she went on holiday?'

'Presumably it was. That's why Molloy picked the place.'

'Isn't it odd that he should be so well informed? He'd only just got out of prison.'

'They learn a lot in those places, don't they?'

'Perhaps. Still it's worth a thought. Oh, and there's a witness statement in there, from the woman in the house that backs on to Number 5.'

'The Judge's wife?' It was indeed Lady Sloper, the wife of the well-known Mr Justice 'Beetle' Sloper, who had got up in the small hours to close a bedroom window. Looking down the moonlit garden of Number 5, she could see, in the clear moonlight, a man come out of the back door. He must have heard her close the window, because he looked up and she got a view of his face. Then she saw him walk away, into the shadows by the garden wall.

'It's a prosecution statement,' Archie explained. 'Freddy Maresfield, who's prosecuting, was good enough to let me see it. They're not calling her, and I shan't be calling her either.'

'Why not? The description she gives doesn't sound in the least like Chirpy Molloy.'

'It was night time . . .'

'Bright moonlight.'

'All the same, she never got a clear view. Freddy would make mincemeat of her in cross-examination. And one doesn't really like to trouble a Judge's wife unless it's absolutely necessary.'

'When it comes to a criminal defence,' I thought it worthwhile to tell Archie Prosser his business, 'it usually pays to trouble everyone as much as possible.'

I had one more question. 'By the way,' I said as Archie reached the door, 'did you ever get round to proposing Bonny Bernard for the Sheridan Club?'

'Oh yes, I did.' Archie clearly didn't get the full implications of my question. 'And he was extremely grateful.'

'Obviously!' My tone was bitter and my brow furrowed with rage, but I let Archie go.

> 'Just for a handful of silver he left us
> Just for a riband to stick in his coat . . .'

He was sitting there, Bonny Bernard, in Pommeroy's Wine Bar, drinking with his partner in the law and, no doubt, in this instance, in crime, the almost anonymous Tillbury; drinking and eating cheese biscuits as though he hadn't been guilty of one of the most appalling acts of treachery in the history of the Bar.

'Oh, hello, Mr Rumpole, you're really looking well.' Bonny Bernard spoke as though all was well with the world and he had nothing on his conscience. The unnecessary Tillbury chipped in with 'Very well indeed, Mr Rumpole. Still at it, are you?'

'I am still at it!' I told them. 'I am still carrying on a practice to the best of my poor ability in Equity Court. All briefs received there marked Mr H. Rumpole will be attended to swiftly and to my usual high standard. But as for you, Bonny Bernard, I'm sorry to have wasted on you the lines written by the poet Browning to the Great Wordsworth, whom he thought a traitor to the cause of human freedom when he sold out and became a civil servant.'

'Really? I didn't know that.' Bernard didn't seem to understand the relevance of the lines to his own conduct. I pointed it out.

'I'm not suggesting you did it for a handful of silver,

Bernard. Perhaps it had more to do with being put up as a member of the Sheridan Club.'

'Oh, yes.' Bernard persisted in behaving as though he had nothing to be ashamed of. 'Your Mr Prosser was kind enough to propose me.'

'So you were kind enough to slip him a brief by way of returning the favour? Do I need to tell you how the poet Browning went on? "He alone sinks to the rear and the slaves!" A slave, I am suggesting, Bernard, to the magnificent prize of becoming a member of a dusty old club. I tell you what. I'll get you into the Bunyan Society. You'll probably recognize Hypocrisy, born in the land of Vainglory.'

'Why don't you sit down, Mr Rumpole?' The unremarkable Tillbury seemed anxious to make peace. 'Can I offer you a drop of the red?'

I sat then, not yet placated, but my outburst had left me thirsty. 'When I think,' I said to Bernard as Tillbury trotted off to the bar, 'of all we've been through together – the business of the Tap End of the Bath murder, the case I called "The Angel of Death". And what about "The Children of the Devil", or "The Puzzling Murder in the Case of Toby Johnson" . . . ?'

'Please, Mr Rumpole, don't go on . . .' Bonny Bernard was, I was glad to see, visibly moved, but I couldn't resist a final turn of the screw. 'And how am I rewarded? My work is transferred to Archie Prosser!'

'Quite honestly, Mr Rumpole, we didn't think you'd want to be bothered.'

Tillbury had arrived with my wine. I downed it and, as usual, the Château Thames Embankment had a calming effect on me. 'I met Chirpy Molloy in prison. His girlfriend's devoted. He means to take up a life of honest toil in her Dad's Videos R Us shop in Lewisham. He instructs you that he never went near Sloane Square on the night in question and

Rumpole and the Primrose Path

his girlfriend Lorraine Hickson provides him with an alibi. If all that's true, Chirpy Molloy is a candidate for redemption. Do you really think I wouldn't be bothered about his case?'

'It seems so open and shut. Nothing much to be done except go through the motions.'

'Seems, Bonny Bernard? I know not seems.' I had given him Browning and John Bunyan. I gave him Hamlet, and all he had given me was a glass of Pommeroy's Very Ordinary in return for a lost brief. 'There are one or two things I might do to help.'

'Things, Mr Rumpole?' Bernard looked vaguely alarmed. 'What sort of things, exactly?'

'Oh, important things. I'm sure Mr Prosser will find them extremely helpful.'

With that I downed a second glass of wine and left Bonny Bernard, who looked as though he were afraid that the trial he'd thought of as 'open and shut' might, with Rumpole on the case, be unexpectedly worrying.

My visit to Worsfield Jail had other results, apart from my meeting with Chirpy Molloy, the prisoner who might or might not have reached a state of redemption. I got a taxi – a sudden, unexpected call to do a plea at London Sessions – and found it to be driven by Vince Timson, one member of the extended family who had, at least for most of the time, a legitimate occupation.

'Great to see you at liberty, Mr Rumpole,' he said. 'Last we saw of you was a picture in the papers when you was entering Worsfield Prison. All the family was upset by that. They really was. "Poor old Mr Rumpole," they said. "They got him at last." Short sentence, was it?'

'Short, but quite unpleasant,' I told him. 'They gave me lunch.'

But I was also given complimentary membership of the Bunyan Society and got a calendar of forthcoming events. The next bash was drinks on the terrace of the House of Lords, when the great and the good, released from lunch in the nick, would be bribed by glasses of champagne and finger food to sign cheques to help the cause of prison reform.

Sunlight glittered on the river and warmed the stone walls of Parliament. The champagne frosted the glasses and the Members, relaxing away from the company of the prisoners the Bunyan Society existed to care for, talked in low, agreeable voices, laughed moderately, nibbled at sausages on sticks or gently introduced fragments of celery into avocado dip. I had brought a guest, none other than Lady Sloper, wife of the Beetle Judge.

'My husband tells me that when you're in a case, Rumpole, he always expects some sort of trouble,' she had told me when I rang her up.

'No sort of trouble now,' I assured her. 'It's just that the Bunyan Society is terribly keen to have you at their drinks party. They've heard you're fantastically interested in prisons.'

'Well, not all that interested, actually. Beetle keeps putting people into them, of course. But my thing's Albanian orphans.'

'Of course it is.' I had tried to sound as though Lady Sloper's work with Albanian orphans was almost the sole topic of conversation round the Old Bailey. 'But if they get here, they quite often end up in prison. For all the wrong reasons, of course. Do say "yes", Lady Sloper. As I say, the Bunyan Society is really desperate to have you.'

'Are they, indeed? And where did you say this party was?'

'Very pleasant surroundings. The terrace of the House of Lords.'

'Really? Well, I do enjoy a party.' Was this a woman, I wondered, who would go anywhere for a samosa and a glass of champagne? 'I don't really see why not.' Lady Sloper, who, reasonably early on, gave me permission to call her Marjorie, was a small, bright-eyed woman, who made good use of the champagne and was licking her fingers after a particularly succulent samosa when she spotted another Judge. 'There's Phillida Erskine-Brown. Beetle really rates her.'

'I think we all do,' I agreed. Across the gently grazing heads I saw the one-time Portia of our Chambers with her QC husband in tow. He was occupying himself by gazing at the other end of the terrace, where the Home Secretary, today in flaming orange with matching earrings, was being chatted up by the top brass of the Bunyan Society. 'Beetle says Phillida Erskine-Brown's top notch on crime, she doesn't stand for any nonsense from you lot saying it's all down to bad parenting or insufficient weaning or whatever.'

'Just as well,' I hastened to agree with Marjorie. 'There's so much of it about nowadays.'

'You mean insufficient weaning?'

'No, I mean crime.' The time had come to bring matters to a head. 'It's everywhere, isn't it? You even saw it from your bedroom window.'

'Well, I saw a man come out of the back door of the house opposite and go off across the garden. Of course, I was the only one who saw it. Beetle was away on circuit.'

'I suppose if he hadn't been he'd have rushed out and collared the fellow.'

'Certainly not. He'd have dug in under the duvet. You obviously don't know my husband.'

'We all have a great deal of respect for Beetle.' I thought it was the right thing to say.

'Oh well, I'm sure he'd be very grateful to you for that.'

Marjorie's affection for the judicial insect fell, it was clear, some degrees short of total adulation.

'You seem to have had a pretty good view of the burglar.'

'You're not defending him, are you?' She looked at me now with some distrust.

'No, not at all,' I reassured her. 'I just happened to read your statement in some papers that got delivered to me by mistake.'

'The prosecution aren't going to call me.' You bet they aren't, I might have said to her, because your description doesn't fit the customer they've decided has, on past performances, got to be guilty. 'Beetle's terribly relieved. He said I'd probably be given a ghastly time by "someone like Rumpole", I have to tell you.' She seemed to find the situation enormously amusing. 'That's exactly what he said.'

'Well, he was wrong,' I promised her. 'I'd have given you the warmest possible welcome. I'd have congratulated you on the clarity of your evidence and your powers of observation. In fact, I'd probably have made you my star witness. That is, if I were doing the case.'

'So it's lucky you aren't,' she told me, 'because I'm not being called at all.'

'Yes, of course. Lucky for someone, anyway.' I looked up the terrace to where the colourful Home Secretary had moved away from the governing group of the Bunyan Society. I took Marjorie up to them. I have to say, I bypassed the mustard-keen director, Katey Kershaw; I merely nodded at the Chairman, Sir James Loveridge. I aimed, with Beetle's wife in tow, straight for the President of the Bunyan, together with the well-heeled Labour peer who had paid for the champagne and canapés. They were being held in no doubt fascinating conversation on prisons and prisoners by the reformed con, Brian Skidmore. I broke, I'm afraid rudely, into their gently murmured conversation to greet Brian. 'You were dead right about Chirpy Molloy,' I congratulated him. 'He couldn't go straight for a month or two. He's right back in the nick on another charge of burglary, with use of bathroom to be taken into consideration.'

Brian smiled knowingly and introduced me to the President and Lord Crane, the Society's benefactor. 'We were talking about an inmate Mr Rumpole met when he had lunch with us in Worsfield.' He brought the top brass up to date with the Molloy affair. 'He's a serial burglar who breaks into people's homes when they're away on holiday and gives himself a bath and uses all the toiletries.'

'What you might call a clean break.' Lord Crane made what had to be the day's worst joke, causing the President to smile indulgently and Brian Skidmore to utter a short yelp of laughter.

'That's a good one, my Lord. A very good one. On a more serious note, though, I knew this chap Molloy hadn't got the strength of character to resist going back to his old ways. Everything's against you when you come out of prison. No money. No job. You meet all the old friends you did crime with . . . It's a hard struggle. I found that. And it needs strength of character.'

'You managed it though, didn't you, Brian?' The President of the Bunyan was smiling proudly.

'Yes, sir, I managed it. But as I say, it wasn't easy. Of course, I had a lot of help from the Bunyan. And I had faith.'

'Religious faith?' Lord Crane sounded doubtful, as though he wasn't sure what particular brand of faith might be under discussion.

'It's what the Bible tells us, isn't it? Whatever sins we might have done – we're all capable of redemption.'

'Pity Chirpy Molloy wasn't,' I agreed with Brian. 'Oh, I'm

so sorry, I forgot to introduce Lady Sloper.' I made the introductions and added, 'By the way, she and the Judge live just behind the house where Chirpy did his last break-in. She was telling me that she saw a man emerge from the back door. Two o'clock in the morning under a full moon. Isn't that right, Lady Sloper?'

But it was hard to get Marjorie's full attention. She had for some time been staring at Brian Skidmore. She was looking, wondering, and I remembered the description of the man she had seen by moonlight, in the statement no one had particularly wanted to be used. A tall man, she had said, with a pronounced nose and a bald dome of a head, which shone hairless in the moonlight. She had seen him clearly until he vanished into the shadows by the garden wall.

Then she answered my question. 'Yes,' she said, 'that's right.'

At this there was a flash of light; behind it, in the shadows, Luci was holding her newly acquired digital camera on which, so she had assured me, she could already see the picture she had taken. Brian Skidmore, the perfect ex-prisoner, however, was having none of it. He snatched Luci's camera from her and stamped on it. 'No photographs!' he shouted, startling the quietly murmuring and grazing guests. 'Didn't anyone tell you? No photographs allowed!' So he left the party, and indeed the Bunyan Society, only to be found, without much difficulty, when he was required to help the police with their enquiries.

In the weeks that followed, I had ample opportunity to consider the doctrine of redemption, as I sat, smoking too many small cigars, not fully employed with briefs calculated to interrupt my train of thought. I did, however, receive several visitors who, in their various ways, threw some light on the subject under consideration. The first of these was Claude Erskine-Brown, who subsided into my client's chair and looked at me with the despairing eyes of a man who can't decide between drowning and an overdose of sleeping pills as the easiest way out of this cruel world.

'Well, Rumpole,' he said, 'it finally happened. At the Bunyan Society do in the House of Lords. You were there, weren't you?'

'Certainly I was there. But what do you mean by "it"?'

'I was speaking,' he said bitterly, 'of the woman who calls herself Home Secretary. She was there, you know.'

'Yes, I know. I saw her. But what I'm groping for, Erskine-Brown, is are you suggesting some sort of consummation?'

'Hardly.' He gave a short laugh which might have been reasonably described as mirthless.

'I thought not. I didn't notice you and the Secretary of State in any sort of clinch behind the potted plants.'

'Of course you didn't. I was there with Philly.'

'Yes, I noticed that. You and the learned Judge.'

'And that woman, Brenda Heygate, came up to us.'

'Smiling?'

'Smiling at Philly. And engaging her in conversation. In fact, she wanted my wife to chair a committee to decide if people should be able to trace the sperm donors who might have fathered them. Yes, Rumpole,' Erskine-Brown's tone became increasingly bitter. 'Sperm donors! That's what they were discussing. Then Philly said to her, "Of course, you know my husband." So this Heygate woman looked at me and do you know what she said?'

'No. Tell me. The suspense is killing me.'

' "No, we've never met." '

'Is that what she said?'

'That's exactly what she said. "No, we've never met." And

she held out her hand for me to shake. I had kissed her, Rumpole! I had seen her to her car and I had kissed her!'

'On the lips?' I was trying to get the picture.

'Partially on the lips. And in part on her cheek. She appeared to enjoy it.'

'I'm sure she did.'

'And now she's saying, "No, we've never met."'

'Perhaps,' I did my best to give him a crumb of comfort, 'she was lying. Wanting to hide her considerable passion.'

'Please! I know you're trying to be kind, Rumpole. She had simply and genuinely forgotten my existence.'

'No doubt she had a good deal on her mind. Affairs of State and all that cracking down.'

'What would Affairs of State matter, if she'd been genuinely in love?'

'I see your point. So what it comes to is – the affair's over?'

'If it ever started.'

'And you can spend more time with your family,' I told him. 'You've been redeemed.'

'I've been what?'

'Redeemed. You might have committed all sorts of sins with the Home Secretary. But now you're a reformed character. You have been granted redemption without even asking for it. Count yourself lucky, Erskine-Brown.'

'If that's redemption,' Claude was lifting himself wearily from my client's chair, 'I'm not sure I care for it at all.'

Some days later, Henry put through a call from my former solicitor, Bonny Bernard. I was delighted to hear him sound as ridden with guilt as any major sinner entering the confessional.

'We've done all you suggested, Mr Rumpole.'

'Good. I'm glad to hear it.' My voice, I hoped, was chilly and the tone curt.

'I've seen Lady Sloper and beefed up her statement. And we're investigating the fingerprint business.'

'Is that all?' I was preparing myself to think of a suitable penance, such as fifty contested careless drivings in the Uxbridge Magistrates' Court, but then the persistent Bernard sprang a surprise.

'I'm sending you a brief, Mr Rumpole.'

'Oh, are you really?' I kept the chill in my voice. 'What is it? Bad case of unrenewed telly licence?'

'No. A murder.'

'Is it indeed?' I couldn't help the voice warming up a little.

'The unusual thing is,' Bernard started to elaborate, 'the death occurred in a Home for the Blind and Partially Sighted.'

'Who's on trial?' I couldn't help asking for further particulars. 'One of the staff?'

'No, actually it's one of the patients. And I think she might have a defence.'

'Send it round then.' A dreadful thought occurred to me. 'I suppose you'll be taking in a leader?'

'No, Mr Rumpole.' My solicitor was admirably clear on this point. 'We thought you'd be better doing this one on your own.'

'Bonny Bernard!' I was then able to tell him, 'I have good news for you. You are a solicitor redeemed.'

I had scarcely slid the tape off the brief in the murder the reformed Bonny Bernard had sent me when, after a brisk knock, Luci Gribble entered the room with a cup of steaming instant. 'That bloody lunatic at the Bunyan,' she said, 'absolutely wrecked my camera. And I was getting some good pics for the Chambers Bulletin.'

'I know.' I was sympathetic. 'He didn't like the sight of his own face.'

I sipped instant, lit a small cigar, but Luci, instead of going, took her place, as so many customers with a guilty secret do, in my client's chair.

'Rumpole,' she said, 'I'm sorry I shopped you like that.'

'Like what, exactly?'

'Well, telling your wife I hadn't noticed you on the exercise bike when I signed you in. I'm afraid I got you into trouble.'

'Trouble? Oh, hardly at all,' I assured her. 'I've been about as welcome in Froxbury Mansions as mice in the larder or a nasty patch of rising damp on the bedroom walls since you grassed about the Lysander Club. That's all. I've had to learn to live with it.'

'I said I'm sorry.'

'That's all right. You told the truth. Some people find doing that an irresistible temptation.'

'But don't worry. I know exactly how you can make up for your shameful neglect of bicycling duty.'

'What are you suggesting?' I was, I have to confess, wary of the Director of Marketing's plans for my future. When it comes to dealing with marriage, the cure is often worse than the disease.

'All you have to do is to remember the date next Thursday.'

'Why?' I was mystified. 'What *is* the date next Thursday?'

'Just look it up and remember it. That's all. By the way, I've booked a table for the two of you at the Myrtle restaurant.'

'You mean . . .' Some distant memory began to trouble my mind.

'Yes. I do mean. It's your wedding anniversary and you're going to take She Who Must Be Obeyed out to dinner.'

'People all talked about Chirpy Molloy leaving his signature on the bathrooms of the houses he burgled. Well, if I know one thing about signatures, it is that they get forged. With all his contacts, the Blessed Saint Brian Skidmore knew all about the jewellery scattered around that house in the Sloane Square area. So he decided to do a job which seemed to have Chirpy's signature written large upon it.'

'Rumpole . . .'

'They were so sure it was Chirpy's work that they didn't bother to look for fingerprints. But when they started looking, they found Brian's on a bottle of Machisimo. He wasn't as careful as Chirpy, you see, and, of course, he never thought anyone would suspect the reformed con with a steady job in the Bunyan Society. He just didn't take enough care.'

'Rumpole, they're taking such a long time with my steak. Do you think they're slaughtering the animal?'

'It's an odd thing about redemption. It seems to come to the most improbable people. Chirpy, it seems, really was redeemed. He'd got his new job and his new girlfriend, and I think he really means to give up invading other people's bathrooms. But the Sainted Brian, exhibit A in the case for prison as a cure for crime, turns out not to have been redeemed at all. Not only did he want to get his fingers on Adele Alexander's baubles, he tried to get a reformed con to do his bird for him.'

'Rumpole, that asparagus wasn't cooked properly. It was hard as nails and had flakes of cheese all over it. It wasn't right, Rumpole. I should have complained at the time.'

'It might have all worked if I hadn't picked up the brief sent to Archie Prosser in a moment of treachery. Well, at least I could organize things so that Prosser could win the case. A somewhat rare event, as I understand it, in the life of our newest arrival in Chambers!'

'Rumpole! Do we have to spend the evening discussing your cases?'

There was a distinct edge to Hilda's voice as she said that. I decided to drop the subject of the forged burglaries.

'No, of course we don't. I mean, why should we discuss my cases? Quite certainly not! By the way, what would you like to discuss?'

'What about – the reason we're here. Dining out. Is that because you're trying to redeem yourself, Rumpole?'

'Yes.' I had to tell her the truth. 'That's what I'm trying to do.'

The Myrtle was packed out as usual that evening; only the networking skills of Luci Gribble had won us a table. Against the dark wood of the walls, over the snowy white tablecloths, the faces, vaguely familiar from Hilda's tabloid and the telly, recognized each other, gave faint little cries of greeting, and then turned their attention back to their plates. Waiters in long white aprons sniffed corks, removed dripping champagne bottles from their buckets or set out plates. It was all far removed from lunch at the Worsfield nick, where this story began. I poured the unaccustomed vintage claret into our glasses and raised mine.

'Happy wedding anniversary.' I touched her glass with mine and took a gulp.

'You remembered?' She Who Must looked as though she didn't believe a word of it.

Again I decided to surprise her with the truth. 'Well, I have to say no, I didn't remember. At least not until Luci reminded me.'

'I told her you never remember.'

'Well, that may be true, as a general rule. But on this occasion Luci told me, and then I remembered it quite clearly.'

'You'd make a hopeless witness, Rumpole.'

'Do you really think so?'

'No one would believe your evidence for a moment.'

'I'm not in the business of giving evidence,' I told her. 'I'm in the business of asking questions.'

'Ask me then.'

'Do I really have to go on bicycling nowhere?'

'You're not going to, are you, whatever I say?'

'No.'

'All right then. I just wanted to keep you going for a little while longer. I can't think why it is, but I don't want to lose you, Rumpole.'

This was so astonishing that it sent me imagining a world without She Who Must Be Obeyed. What would it be like? I seemed to see a great emptiness. A world without difficult cases, as bland, perhaps, as a world without crime or the possibility of redemption. I was about to say something along these lines when the waiter arrived and slid her main course dexterously in front of Hilda. She switched her attention from me to the waiter.

'I hope it's as I like it,' she said. 'By the way, I think I should tell you, the asparagus was not right.'

'Not right?' The waiter was Australian and took Hilda's complaint with a cheerful smile.

'To begin with it was hard as nails. I almost broke my teeth on it.'

'That's right! Al dente.'

'Well, we can do without the al dente, thank you. And someone had put bits of cheese on it.'

'Parmesan.'

'Exactly! So you admit it. You don't put cheese on asparagus. It wasn't right, you know. I'd like you to know that, because we're quite likely to be back at the same time next year.'